The Penniless Lords

In want of a wealthy wife

Meet Daniel, Gabriel, Lucien and Francis
Four lords, each down on his fortune and
each in need of a wife of means.

From such beginnings, can these marriages of
convenience turn into something
more treasured than money?

Don't miss this enthralling new quartet by
Sophia James

Read Daniel, Gabriel, Lucien
and Francis's stories in

Marriage Made in Money
Already available

Marriage Made in Shame
Already available

Marriage Made in Rebellion
Out now

Marriage Made in Hope
Coming soon

She tasted like hope and home.

And of something else entirely.

Tristesse.

The French word for sadness came from nowhere, bathed in its own truth, but it was too soon to pay good mind to it and too late to want it different.

'Only now, Lucien,' she whispered. 'I know it is all that each of us can promise, but it is enough.'

MARRIAGE MADE IN REBELLION

Sophia James

Published in Great Britain 2016
By Mills & Boon, an imprint of HarperCollins*Publishers*
1 London Bridge Street, London, SE1 9GF

© 2016 Sophia James

ISBN: 978-0-263-91677-5

Printed and bound in Spain
by CPI, Barcelona

Sophia James lives in Chelsea Bay, on Auckland, New Zealand's North Shore, with her husband, who is an artist. She has a degree in English and History from Auckland University and believes her love of writing was formed by reading Georgette Heyer in the holidays at her grandmother's house. Sophia enjoys getting feedback at sophiajames.co.

Books by Sophia James

Mills & Boon Historical Romance

The Penniless Lords

Marriage Made in Money
Marriage Made in Shame
Marriage Made in Rebellion

Men of Danger

Mistletoe Magic
Mistress at Midnight
Scars of Betrayal

The Wellingham Brothers

High Seas to High Society
One Unashamed Night
One Illicit Night
The Dissolute Duke

Stand-Alone Novels

Knight of Grace
Lady with the Devil's Scar
Gift-Wrapped Governesses
'Christmas at Blackhaven Castle'

Visit the Author Profile page
at millsandboon.co.uk for more titles.

Author Note

Marriage Made in Rebellion is the third story in my The Penniless Lords series.

Lucien Howard, the Earl of Ross, is a soldier, a fighter, a spy and a gifted linguist.

Alejandra Fernandez y Santo Domingo is the only daughter of a powerful Spanish guerrilla leader whose family has been decimated by the conflict.

They come together on the battlefields after Corunna in this dark and dangerous story of high-stakes warfare in a country that has been split apart by politics. It is also about a great love that conquers all.

Francis St Cartmail is next. When Lady Sephora Connaught falls from a bridge into the deep and fast-running Thames everything in her world changes.

The stranger who dives in to rescue her, the Earl of Douglas, is known as the black sheep of the *ton* and is a man of questionable reputation. Yet only with him does she finally feel safe.

I love feedback, and you can find me at sophiajames.co.

Chapter One

The English declare they will no longer respect neutrals on the sea; I will no longer recognise them on land.

Napoleon Bonaparte

A Coruña, Spain—January 16th, 1809

Captain Lucien Howard, the Earl of Ross, thought his nose was broken. His neck, too, probably, because he couldn't move it at all. His horse lay upon him, her head bent sideways and liquid-brown eyes empty of life. A good mare she was, one that had brought him up the hard road from Lisboa through the snows of the Cantabrian Mountains and the slippery passways of mud and sleet. He swore silently and looked away.

It hurt to breathe, a worrying thought that, given the distance from any medical help. Another day and Napoleon and his generals would be all over the harbour. It was finished and the British had lost, the harsh winter eating into what was left of resistance and a mix-up with the ocean transports in from the southern port of Vigo.

God, if he wasn't so badly hurt, he might have laughed, but the movement would have most likely killed him. It was so damn cold, his breath fogging as he fought for what little air he could drag in, but a mist had come up from the sea to mingle with the smoke of battle hanging thick across the valley.

Lucien was not afraid of death. It was the dying that worried him, the length and the breadth of it and the helplessness.

Lying back, he looked up into the heavens, hoping that it would be quick. He couldn't pray; that sort of hope was long since past and had been for a while now. He could not even find the words to ask for forgiveness or penance. He had killed men, good and bad, in the name of king and country, but once one saw the whites of an enemy's eyes, the old troths and promises held less sway than they once had.

A man was a man whatever language he spoke and more often than not a family would be waiting at home for their return. As his was. That thought sent a shaft of pain through the greater ache, but, resolving not to die with tears in his eyes, Lucien willed it away.

It was late, that much he did know, the sun deep on the horizon and only a little left of the day. He could see the lights of resin torches further away along the lines of the olive trees and the aloe hedges, searching for those who still lived. He could not summon the strength to call out as he lay there, a rough stone wall to one side and an old garden of sorts on the other.

Lucien imagined he could smell orange blossoms and wild flowers, but that was surely wrong. He wondered about the warmth that he felt as the peace of a contrition he long since should have made came unexpectedly.

'Forgive me, Jesus, for I have sinned.' Not so hard now in the final moments of his life. He smiled. No, not so hard at all.

The English soldier was covered in the blood of his horse, the residual warmth left in the large animal's pelt saving him, allowing him life in the frigid cold dark dawn of a Galician January winter.

But not for long; his blond hair was pinked in a puddle of blood beneath his head and a wound at his neck wept more. The daybreak was sending its first light across the sky and as far as the eye could see there were bodies. English and French, she thought, entwined in death like friends. Only the generals could have imagined that such a sacrifice was worth it, the prime of each country gone before they had ever had the chance to live. She cursed out loud against the futility of war and removed the gold signet ring from the soldier's finger to give to her father.

When his eyes flicked open the pale in them was startling in the early-morning light, almost see-through.

'Not…dead…yet?' There was disappointment and resignation in the broken question phrased in Spanish.

'What hurts?'

He smiled. 'What…does…not?'

The wide planes of his cheeks were bruised and his lip was badly cut, but even with the marks of war drawn from one end of him to the other he was beautiful; too beautiful to just die here unheralded and forgotten. Anger fortified resolve and she slashed at the gorse to one side of him, using the cleared ground to stand upon.

With space she pried a broken stake from a fence under his mount's neck and managed to lift it up enough, twisting the carcass so that it fell away from him, swirls of mud staining the air.

He groaned, the noise one makes involuntarily when great pain breaks through a consciousness that cannot quite contain it.

'Scream away, Ingles, if you will,' she told him. 'I most certainly would. Your friends have been evacuated by way of the sea and the French are in charge of the township itself, so nobody at all should hear you.'

My God, how tired she was of iron wills and masculine stoicism. Death was a for ever thing and if men taking their last breaths in a land far from their own could not weep for the sacrifice, then who else should?

Not her. Not her father. Not the officers safe with their horses on the transports home across a wild and stormy Biscay Bay. Other steeds roamed the streets of A Coruña, looking for succour, their more numerous and unluckier counterparts dead beneath the cliffs overhanging the beach, throats cut in clumsy acts of kindness.

Better dead than at the mercy of the enemy. Once she might have even believed that truism. Now she failed to trust in anything or anyone. The fury within alarmed her at times, but mostly she did not think on it. Adan and Bartolomeu had joined her now, their canvas stretcher pulled in.

'You want us to take him back?'

She nodded. 'Careful how you lift him.'

As Tomeu crouched down he scratched at a muddied epaulette. 'He's a *capitán*.' The tinged gold was undeniable and her heart sank. Her father had begun to be uncertain of a Spanish triumph and was distancing himself from the politics of the region. An officer would be less welcome than a simple soldier to Enrique. More complex. Harder to explain.

'Then we need to make sure he recovers to fight again for our cause.'

For some reason the man before her was beginning to mean something. A portent to victory or a prophecy of failure? She could not tell. All she did know was that the damaged fingers of his left hand had curled into her own, seeking comfort, and that despite all intentions to do otherwise she held them close, trying to bring warmth to his freezing skin.

He groaned again when they rolled him on to the canvas and she got the first glimpse of the wounds on his upper back, the fabric of his shirt shredded into slivers and the flesh hanging off him between it.

More than one sword had been used, she thought, and there had been a good deal of hatred in the action. The blood loss was making him shake, so she shrugged off her woollen poncho and laid it across him, tucking it in beneath his chin.

Tomeu looked up with a frown. 'Why bother? He will die anyway.' The hard words of truth that she did not want, though there was anger in his tone, too. 'They come and they go. In the end it's all the same. Death eats them up.'

'Padre Nuestro que estás en los cielos...' She recited the Lord's Prayer beneath her breath and draped the ornate rosary across him in protection as they started for home.

* * *

The same lad on the fields was beside him again, sitting asleep on a chair, a hat pulled down over his face. Lucien shook his head against the chills that were consuming him and wondered where the hell he was. Not on the battlefields, not on the transports home, either, and this certainly was not hell given the crisp cotton sheets and warm woollen blanket.

Tipping his head, he tried to listen to the cadence of someone speaking far away outside. Spanish. He was certain of it. The heavy beams and whitewashed walls told him this house was also somewhere in the Iberian Peninsula and that whoever owned it was more than wealthy.

His eyes flicked back to the lad. Young. Thin. A working boy. Lucien could not quite understand what he would be doing here. Why was he not labouring somewhere or helping with one of the many things that would need attention on a large and busy hacienda? What master would allow him simply to sit in a sickroom whiling away the hours?

His glance caught the skin of an ankle above a weathered and scuffed boot, though at that very moment deep green eyes opened, a look of interest within them.

'You are awake?'

A dialect of León, but with an inflection that he didn't recognise.

'Where am I?' He answered in the same way and saw surprise on the lad's brow.

'Safe.' Uttered after a few seconds of thought.

'How long…here?'

'Three days. You were found on the battle-field above A Coruña the morning after the English had departed by way of the sea.'

'And the French?'

'Most assuredly are enjoying the spoils of war. Soult has come into the town with his army under Napoleon's orders, I suppose. There are many of them.'

'God.'

At that the lad crossed himself, the small movement caught by the candlelight a direct result of his profanity.

'Who are you?' This question was almost whispered.

'Captain Howard of the Eighteenth Light Dragoons. Do you have any news of the English general Sir John Moore?'

'They buried him at night on the high ground close to the ramparts of the Citadel. It is told he died well with his officers around him. A cannon shot to the chest.'

Pain laced through Lucien. 'How do you know this?'

'This is our land, Capitán. The town is situated less than three miles from where we are and there is little that happens in the region that we are not aware of.'

'We.'

The silence was telling.

'You are part of the guerrilla movement? One of El Vengador's minions? This is his area of jurisdiction, is it not?'

The boy ignored that and gave a question of his own. 'Where did you learn your Spanish?'

'Five months in Spain brings its rewards.'

'But not such fluency.' The inflection of disbelief was audible.

'I listen well.'

In the shadows of a slender throat Lucien saw the pulse quicken and a hand curl to a fist. A broken nail and the remains of a wound across the thumb. Old injuries. Fragile fingers. Delicate. Tentative. Left-handed. There was always so much to learn from the small movements.

She was scared of him.

The pronoun leapt into a life of its own. It was the ankles, he was to think later, and the utter thinness of her arms.

'Who are you, *señorita*?'

She stood at that, widening one palm across the skin on his neck and pressing down. 'If you say one word of these thoughts to anyone else, you will be dead, *desconocido*, before you have the chance to finish your sentence. Do you understand?'

He looked around. The door was closed and the walls were thick. 'You did not…save my life…to kill me…now.'

He hoped he was right, because there was no more breath left. When she let him go he hated the relief he felt as air filled his lungs. To care so much about living made him vulnerable.

'The others will not be so lenient of your conjectures were you to utter them carelessly and everybody here would protect me with their life.'

He nodded and looked away from the uneasy depths of green.

'I take it, then, that you are the daughter of

this house.' He had changed his accent now into a courtly High Castilian and saw her stiffen, but she did not answer and was gone before he could say another word.

Who the hell was he, this stranger with the pale blue eyes that saw everything, his hair like spun gold silk and a body marked by war?

No simple soldier, that much was certain. The Light Dragoons had fought with Paget out of San Cristobel and yet he had been found east of Piedralonga, a good two miles away under Hope's jurisdiction. She frowned in uncertainty.

Captain Howard had spoken in the León dialect and then in the Castilian, easily switching. A changeling who could be dangerous to them all and it was she who had brought him here. She should say something of the worrying contradictions to her father and the others. She should order him removed and left far from the hacienda to fend for himself. But instead…

Instead she walked to the windows of her room and looked out across the darkness to the sea beyond. There was something about this *capitán* that she recognised in herself. An interloper isolated from others and surrounded by danger. He did not show fear, either, for when she had taken the air from his windpipe with her hands he had not fought her. But waited. As if he had known she would let go.

Cursing, she pulled the shutters in closed against the night.

Lucien lay awake and listened. To the gentle swish of a servant's skirt and then the harder steps of someone dousing the lights outside. A corridor by the sounds of it and open to the sea. When his rescuer passed without he had smelt the salt and heard the waves crashing against the shore. Three miles she had said to A Coruña and yet here the sea was closer, a mile at the most and less if the wind drew from the north as it had done three days ago. Now the breeze was lighter for there was no sound at all against the wood of the shutters. Heavy locks pulled the coverings together in three places and with a patina of age Lucien knew these to be old bindings. To one side of the thick lintels of double-sashed windows he saw scratches in the limewash over stone, lines carefully kept in groups. Days of the week? Hours of a day? Months of a year? He could not quite make them out from this distance.

Why had these been left there? A servant could have been ordered to cover them in the matter of a few moments; a quick swish of thick plaster and they would have been gone.

A Bible sat on a small wooden table next to his bed under an ornate golden cross and beside a bronze statue of Jesus with his crown of thorns.

Catholic and devout.

Lucien felt akin to the battered Christ, as his neck ached and sharp pains raked up his back. The sword wounds from the French as he had tried to ride in behind the ranks of General Hope. He was hot now, the pins and needles of fever in his hands, and his front tooth ached badly, but he was too tired to bring his arm up enough to touch the damage. He wished the thin girl would come back to give him some more water and sit near him, but only the silence held court.

She returned in the morning, before the silver dawn had changed to day, and this time she brought others.

The man beside her was nearing fifty, Lucien imagined, a big man wearing the flaring scarlet-and-light-blue jacket of an Estramaduran hussar. Two younger men accompanied him.

'I am Señor Enrique Fernandez y Castro, otherwise known as El Vengador, Capitán. It seems you have heard of me?'

Lucien sized up the hard dark eyes and the generous moustache of the guerrilla leader. A man of consequence in these parts and feared because of it. He looked nothing at all like his daughter.

'If the English soldiers do not return, there will be little hope for the Spanish cause, Capitán.' High Castilian. There was no undercurrent of any lesser dialect in his speech but the pure and arrogant notes of aristocracy.

Lucien was honest in his own appraisal of the situation. 'Well, the Spanish generals have done themselves no favour, *señor*, and it's lucky the French are in such disorder. If Napoleon himself had taken the trouble to be in the Iberian Peninsula, instead of leaving it to his brother, I doubt anything would be left.'

The older man swore. 'Spain has no use for men who usurp a crown and the royal Bourbons are powerless to fight back. It is only the likes of the partisans that will throw the French from España, for the army, too, is useless in its fractured purpose.'

Privately Lucien agreed, but he did not say so. The *juntas* were splintered and largely ineffective. John Moore and the British expeditionary force had found that out the hard way, the promise of a Spanish force of men never eventuating, but sliding away into quarrel.

The girl was listening intently, her eyes wary beneath the rim of the same cap she had worn each time he had seen her. Today the jacket was different, though. Something stolen from an English foot soldier, he guessed, the scarlet suiting her tone of skin. He flipped his glance from her as quickly as it settled. She had given him her warnings already and he owed her that much.

The older man moved back, the glint of metal in his leather belt. 'Soult and Ney are trampling over the north as we speak, but the south is still free.'

'Because the British expeditionary forces dragged any opposition up here with them as they came.'

'Perhaps,' the other man agreed, dark eyes thoughtful. 'How is it you know our language so well?'

'I was in Dominica for a number of years before coming to Madeira.'

'The dialects would be different.' The room was still, waiting, a sense of menace and distrust covering politeness.

For the first time in days Lucien smiled. 'Every tutor I had said I was gifted in hearing the cadence of words and I have been in Spain for a while.'

'Why were you found behind the English lines? The Eighteenth Dragoons were miles away. Why were you not there with them?'

'I was scouting the ocean for the British transports under the direction of General Moore. They were late coming into the harbour and he was worried.'

'A spy, then.'

'I myself prefer the title of intelligence officer.'

'Semantics.' The older man laughed, though, and the tension lessened.

When Lucien chanced a look at the girl he saw she watched him with a frown across her brow. Today there was a bruise on her left cheek that was darkening into purple. It had not been there yesterday.

Undercurrents.

The older man was not pleased by Lucien's presence in the house and the Catalan *escopeta* in his cartouche belt was close. One wrong word could decide Lucien's fate. He stayed silent whilst he tried to weigh up his options and he listened as the other man spoke.

'Every man and woman in Spain is armed with a flask of poison, a garrotting cord or a knife. Napoleon is not the liberator here and his troops will not triumph. The Treaty of Tilsit was his star as its zenith, but now the power and the glory have begun to fade. *C'est le commencement de la fin*, Capitán, and the French know it.'

'Something Talleyrand said, I think? Hopefully prophetic.' Lucien had heard rumours that the crafty French bishop was seeking to negotiate a secure peace behind his emperor's back so as to perpetuate and solidify the gains made during the French revolution.

El Vengador stepped forward. 'You are well informed. But our channels of intelligence are healthy, too, and one must watch what one utters to a stranger, would you not agree, Capitán? Best to hold your secrets close.'

And your enemies closer? A warning masked beneath the cloth of politics? Simple. Intimidating. Lucien resisted any urge to once again glance at his rescuer in the corner.

He nodded without candour and was relieved as the other man moved back.

'You will be sent by boat to England. Tomeu will take you. But I would ask something of you before you leave us. Your rank will allow you access to the higher echelons of the English military and we need to know the intentions of the British parliament's actions against the French here in Spain. Someone will contact you wearing this.' He brought a ruby brooch out of his pocket to show him, the gem substantial and the gold catching the light. 'Any information you can gather would be helpful. Sometimes it is the very smallest of facts that can make a difference.'

And with that he was gone, leaving his daughter behind as the others departed with him.

'He trusts you.' Her words came quietly. 'He

would not have let this meeting run on for as long as it has if he did not.'

'He knows I know about…?' One hand gestured towards her.

'That I am a girl? Indeed. Did you not hear his warning?'

'Then why did he leave you here? Now?'

At that she laughed. 'You cannot guess, Capitán?' Her green eyes glittered with the look of one who knew her worth. To the cause. To her father. To the machinations of a guerrilla movement whose very lifeblood depended on good information and loyal carriers.

'Hell. It is you he will send?'

'A woman can move in many circles that a man cannot.' There was challenge in her words as she lifted her chin and the swollen mark on her cheek was easier to see.

'Who hit you?'

'In a place of war, emotions can run high.'

For the first time in his company she blushed and he caught her left hand. The softness of her skin wound around his warmth.

'How old are you?'

'Nearly twenty-three.'

'Old enough to know the dangers of subterfuge, then? Old enough to realise that men might not all be…kind?'

'You warn me of the masculine appetite?'

'That is one way of putting it, I suppose.'

'This is Spain, Capitán, and I am hardly a green girl.'

'You are married?'

She did not answer.

'You were married, but he is dead.'

Horror marked her face. 'How could you possibly know that?'

With care he extended her palm and pointed to her third finger. 'The skin is paler where you once wore a ring. Just here.'

She felt the lump at the back of her throat hitch up into fear. She felt other things, too, things she had no mandate to as she wrenched away from his touch and went to stand by the window, the blood that throbbed at her temples making her feel slightly sick.

'How are you called? By your friends?'

'Lucien.'

'My mother named me Anna-Maria, but my father never took to it. He changed it when I was five and I became Alejandra, the defender of mankind. He did not have another child, you see.'

'So the boy he had always wanted was lost to him and you would have to do?'

She was shocked by his insight. 'You can see such a truth in my father's face just by looking at him?'

The pale eyes narrowed as he shook his head. 'He allows you to dress as a boy and roam the dangerous killing fields of armies. He will have trained you, no doubt, in marksmanship and in the using of a knife, but you are small and thin and this is a perilous time and place for any woman.'

'What if I told you that such patronage works to my advantage, Capitán? What if I said you think like all the others and dismiss the mouse against the lion?'

His glance went to her cheek.

'I broke his wrist.' When he smiled the wound on his lip stretched and blood blossomed.

'Why did he hurt you?'

'He felt the English should be left to rot in the arms of the enemy because of the way they betrayed us by departing in such an unseemly haste.'

'A harsh sentiment.'

'My father believes it, too, but then every war comes with a cost that you of all people should know of. The doctor said your back will be marked for good.'

'Are you suggesting that I will survive?'

'You thought you wouldn't?'

'Without you I am certain of it.'

'There is still time to die, Capitán. The sea trip won't be comfortable and inflammation and fever are always possibilities with such deep lacerations.'

'Your bedside manner is lacking, *señorita*. One usually offers more hope when tending a helpless patient.'

'You do not seem vulnerable in any way to me, Capitán Howard.'

'With my back cut to ribbons…?'

'Even with that. And you have been hurt before. Madeira or Dominica were dangerous places, then?'

'Hardly. Our regiment was left to flounder and rot in the Indies because no politician ever thought to abandon the rich islands.'

'For who in power should be brave enough to risk money for justice?'

He laughed. 'Who indeed?'

Alejandra turned away from his smile. He surely must know how beautiful he was, even with his ruined lip and swollen eye. He should have been weeping with the pain from the wounds at his neck and back and yet here he lay, scanning the room and its every occupant for clues and for the answers to questions she could see in his pale blue eyes. What would a man like this be like when he was well?

As unbeatable and dangerous as her father.

The answer almost had her turning away, but she made herself stand still.

'My father believes that the war here in the Peninsula will drag on for enough years to kill many more good men. He says it is Spain that will determine the outcome of the emperor's greed and this is the reason he has fashioned himself into the man he has become. El Vengador. The Avenger. He no longer believes in the precise and polite assignations of armies. He is certain that triumph lies in darker things; things like the collation of gathered information and night-time raids.'

'And you believe this, too? It is why you would come to England wearing your ruby brooch?'

'Once upon a time I was another person, Capitán. Then the French murdered my mother and I joined my father's cause. Revenge is what shapes us all here now and you would be wise to keep that in mind.'

'When did she die?'

'Nearly two years ago, but it seems like a lifetime. My father adored her to the exclusion of all else.'

'Even you?'

Again that flash of anger, buried quickly.

He turned away, the ache of his own loss in his thoughts. Were his group of army guides safe or had they been left behind in the scramble for transports?

He had climbed the lighthouse called the Tower of Hercules a dozen times or more to watch for the squadron to appear across the grey and cold Atlantic Ocean. But the transports and their escorts had not come until the eleventh hour, all his intelligence suggesting that French general Soult was advancing and that the main body of their army was not far behind.

He thought of John and Philippe and Hans and Giuseppe and all the others in his ragtag bag of deserters and ne'er-do-wells; a group chosen for their skill in languages and for their intuition. He had trained them and honed them well, every small shred of intelligence placed into the fabric of a whole, to be deciphered and collated and acted upon.

Communication was the lifeblood of an army and it had been his job to see that each message was delivered and every order and report was followed up. Sometimes there was more. An intercepted cache from the French, a dispatch that had fallen into hands it should not have or a personal letter of inestimable value.

His band of guides was an exotic mix of nationalities only vaguely associated with the English army and he was afraid of what might happen to them if they had been left behind.

'Were there many dead on the field where you found me?'

'There were. French and English alike. But there would have been more if the boats had not come into the harbour. The inhabitants of A Coruña sheltered the British well as they scampered in ragged bands to the safety of the sea.'

Then that was that. Every man would have to take their chance at life or death because he could do nothing for any of them and his own future, as it was, was hanging in the balance.

He could feel the heat in him and the tightness, the sensation of nothingness across his shoulders and back worrying. His left hand was cursed again with a ferocious case of pins and needles and his stomach felt…hollow.

He smiled and the girl opposite frowned, seeing through him perhaps, understanding the pretence of it.

He hadn't been hungry, any slight thought of food making him want to throw up. He had been drinking, though, small sips of water that wet his mouth and burnt the sores he could feel stretched over his lips.

A sorry sight, probably. He only wished he could be sick and then, at least, the gall of loss might be dislodged. Or not.

'You have family?'

A different question, almost feminine.

'My mother and four siblings. There were eight of us before my father and youngest brother were drowned.'

'A big number, then. Sometimes I wish…' She stopped at that and Lucien could see a muscle under her jaw grinding from the echo of words.

Nothing personal. Nothing particular. It was how this aftermath of war and captivity worked, for anything could be used against anyone in the easy pickings of torture. His own voluntary admissions of family worked in another way, a shared communion, a bond of humanness. Encourage dialogue with a captor and foster friendship. The enemy was much less likely to kill you then.

Fortunes turned on an instant and any thinking man or woman in this corner of a volatile Spain would know that. Battles were won and then lost and won again. It was only time that counted and with three hundred thousand fighting men of France poised at your borders and under the control of Napoleon Bonaparte himself there was no doubt of the outcome.

Unless England and its forces returned and

soon, Spain would go the way of nearly every other free land in Europe.

His head ached at the thought.

The girl came back to read to him the next afternoon and the one after that, her voice rising and falling over the words of the first part of Miguel de Cervantes's tale *Don Quixote*.

Lucien had perused this work a number of times and he thought she had, too, for there were moments when she looked up and read from memory.

He liked listening to her voice and he liked watching her, the exploits of the eccentric and hapless Knight of La Mancha bringing deep dimples to both of her cheeks. She used her free hand a lot, too, he saw, in exclamation and in emphasis, and when the edge of her jacket dipped he saw a number of white scars drawn across the dark blue of her blood line at her wrist.

As she finished the book she snapped the covers together and leant back against the wide leather chair, watching him. 'The pen is the language of the soul, would you not agree, Capitán?'

He could not help but nod. 'Cervantes, as a soldier, was seized for five years. All good fodder for his captive's tale, I suppose.'

'I did not know that.'

'Perhaps that is where he first conjured up the madness of his hero. The uncertainty of captivity forces questions and makes one re-evaluate priorities.'

'Is it thus with you?'

'Indeed. A prisoner always wonders whether today is the day he holds no further use alive to those who keep him bound.'

'You are not a prisoner. You are here because you are sick. Too sick to move.'

'My door is locked, Alejandra. From the outside.'

That disconcerted her, a frown appearing on her brow as she glanced away. 'Things are not always as they seem,' she returned and stood. 'My father isn't a man who would kill you for no reason at all.'

'Is expedience enough of a reason? Or plain simple frustration? He wants me gone. I am a nuisance he wishes he did not have.' Lifting his hand, he watched it shake. Violently.

'Then get better, damn you.' Her words were

threaded with the force of anger. 'If you can walk to the door, you can get to the porch. And if you can manage that, then you can go further and further again. Then you can leave.'

In answer he reached for the Bible by his bed and handed it to her. 'Like this man did?'

Puzzled, she opened the book to the page indicated by the plaited golden thread of a bookmark.

Help me. I forgive you.

Written shakily in charcoal, the dust of it blurred in time and use and mirrored on the opposite page. When her eyes went to the lines etched in the whitewash beneath the window on the opposite wall Lucien knew exactly what the marks represented.

'He was a prisoner in this room, too?'

She crossed herself, her face frozen in pain and shock and deathly white.

'You know nothing, Capitán. Nothing at all. And if you ever mention this to my father even once, he will kill you and I won't be able to stop him.'

'You would try?'

The air about them stilled into silence, the

dust motes from the old fabric on the Bible twirling in the light, a moment caught for ever. And he fell into the green of her unease without resistance, like a moth might to flame in the darkest of nights.

She was the most beautiful woman he had ever seen, but it was not that which drew him. It was her strength of emotion, the anger in her the same as that in him. She balanced books and a blade with an equal dexterity, the secrets in her eyes wound into both sadness and knowledge.

They were knights tilting at windmills in the greater pageant of a Continental war, the small hope of believing they might make a difference lost under the larger one of nationalistic madness.

Spain. France. England.

For the first time in his life Lucien questioned the wisdom of soldiering and the consequences of battle, for them all, and came up wanting.

Alejandra had known the man who had written this message, he was sure of it, and it had shocked her. The pulse in her throat was still heightened as she licked her lips against the dryness of fear.

He watched as she ripped the page from the Bible before giving the tome back to him, tearing the age-thin paper into small pieces and pocketing them.

The weight of the book in his fist was heavy as she turned and left the room.

God. In the ensuing silence he flicked through the pages and his eyes again found a further passage marked in charcoal amongst the teachings of the Old Testament. Matthew 6:14. *'For if you forgive men when they sin against you, your heavenly father will also forgive you.'*

Clearly Alejandra, daughter of El Vengador, sought neither forgiveness nor absolution. Lucien wondered why.

He woke much later, startled into consciousness by great pain, and she was there again, sitting on the chair near the bed and watching him. The Bible had been removed altogether now, he noted as he chanced a glance at the table by the bed.

'The doctor said you had to drink.'

He tried to smile. 'Brandy?'

Her lips pursed as she raised a glass of orange-and-mint syrup. 'This is sweetened and the honey will help you to heal.'

'Thank you.' Sipping at the liquid, he enjoyed the coolness as it slid down his throat.

'Don't take too much,' she admonished. 'You will not be used to much yet.'

He frowned as he lay back, the dizziness disconcerting. If he did lose the contents of his stomach, he was almost certain it would not be Alejandra who would be offering to clean it up. He swallowed heavily and counted to fifty.

After a few moments she spoke again. 'Are you a religious man, Capitán Howard?'

A different question from what he had expected. 'I was brought up in the Anglican faith, but it's been a while since I was in any church.'

'When faith is stretched the body suffers.' She gave him this as though she had read it somewhere, a sage piece of advice that she had never forgotten.

'I think it is the French who have more to do with my suffering, *señorita*.'

'Ignoring the power of God's healing in your position could be dangerous. A priest could give you absolution should you wish it.' There was anger in her words.

'No.' He had not meant it to sound so final. 'If I die, I die. If I don't, I don't.'

'Fate, you mean? You believe in such?'

'I do believe in a fate that falls on men unless they act. The prophet Buddha said something like that a very long time ago.'

She smiled. 'Your religion is eclectic, then? You take bits from this deity and then from that one? To suit your situation?'

He looked away from her because he could tell she thought his answer important and he didn't have the strength to explain that it had been a while since he had believed in anything at all.

The shutters hadn't been closed tonight at his request and the first light of a coming dawn was low on the horizon. He was gladdened to see the beginning of another day. 'Do you not sleep well? To be here at this time?'

'Once, I did. Once, it was hard to wake me from a night's slumber, but since…' She stopped. 'No. I do not sleep well any more.'

'Is there family in other places, safer places than here?'

'For my father to send me to, you mean?' She stood and blew out the candle near his bed. 'I need no looking after, *señor*. I am quite able to see to myself.'

Shadowed against the dying night she looked smaller than usual, as if in the finding of the words in the Bible earlier some part of her had been lost.

'Fate can also be a kind thing, *señor*. There is a certain grace in believing that nothing one does will in the end make any difference to what finally happens.'

'Responsibility, you mean?'

'Do not discount it completely, Capitán. Guilt can eat a soul up with barely a whisper.'

'So you are saying fate is like a pardon because all free will is gone?'

Even in the dim light he could see her frown.

'I am saying that every truth has shades of lies within and one would be indeed foolish to think it different.'

'Like the words you tore from the Bible? The ones written in charcoal?'

'Especially those ones,' she replied, a

strength in the answer that had not been there a moment ago. 'Those words were a message he knew I would find.'

With that she was gone, out into the early coming dawn, the shawl at her shoulders tucked close around her chin.

Chapter Two

Alejandra watched Captain Lucien Howard out amongst the shadow of trees on the pathway behind the hacienda: one step and then falling, another and falling again. He had insisted on being brought outside each day, one of the servants carrying him to the grove so that he could practise walking.

She could see frustration, rage and pain in every line of his body from this distance and the will to try to stand unaided, even as the dust had barely settled from the previous unsuccessful attempt. His hands would be bleeding, she knew that without even looking, for the bark of the olive was rough and he had needed traction to pull his whole weight up in order to stand each time. Sickness and fever had left him wasted and thin. The man they had brought up from the battlefields of A Coruña had been twice the one he was now.

Another Englishman who had shed his blood on the fleshless bones of this land, a land made bare by war and hate and greed. She turned her rosary in her palm, reciting the names of those who had died already. Rosalie. Pedro. Even Juan with his cryptic and unwanted whine of forgiveness written in a Bible he knew she would find.

Each bead was smooth beneath her fingers, a hundred years of incantations ingrained in the shining jet. Making the sign of the cross, she kept her voice quiet as she prayed. 'I believe in God, the Father Almighty, Creator of Heaven and Earth and…'

Salvation came in many forms and this was one of them, the memory of those gone kept for ever present within the timeless words. After the Apostles' Creed she started on the Our Father, following it with three Hail Marys, a Glory Be and the Fatima Prayer.

She always used the Sorrowful Mysteries now as a way to end her penance, the Joyful and the Glorious ones sticking in her throat; the Agony in the Garden and the Crowning of the Thorns were more relevant to her life these days. Even the Scourging of the Pillars appealed.

When she had finished she placed the beads in her left pocket, easily reached, and drew out a knife from the leather pouch at her ankle, the edge of it honed so that it gleamed almost blue.

A small branch of an aloe hedge lay beside her and she lifted the wood against the blade, sliding the knife so that shavings fell in a pile around her boots.

Her life was like this point of sharp, balanced on a small edge of living. Turning the stick, she drew it down against her forearm, where the skin held it at bay for a moment in a fleeting concave show of resistance.

With only the smallest of pressure she allowed the wood to break through, taking the sudden pain inside her, not allowing even a piece of it to show.

Help me. I forgive you. A betrayal written in charcoal.

Blood welled and ran in a single small stream across her hands and on to her fingertips, where it fell marking the soil.

Sometimes pain was all she had left to feel

with, numbness taking everything else. If she were honest, she welcomed the ache of life and the flow of blood because in such quickness she knew she was still here. Still living. Just.

Lucien Howard had almost fallen again and she removed the point from her arm, staunching the wound with pressure, setting blood.

He was like her in his stubbornness, this captain. Never quite giving up. Resheathing the blade, she simply leant back and shut her eyes, feeling the thin morning sun against her lids and the cold wind off the Atlantic across her hair.

Her land. For ever.

She would never leave it. The souls of those long departed walked beside her here. Already mud was reclaiming her blood. She liked to think it was her mother, Rosalie, there in the whorls of wind, drinking her in, caressing the little that was left, understanding her need for aloneness and hurt.

Her eyes caught a faster movement. Now the Englishman had gone down awkwardly and this time he stayed there. She counted the seconds under her breath. One. Two. Three. Four.

Then a quickening. A hand against the tree.

The pull of muscle and the strain of flesh. Her fingers lifted to find the rosary, but she stopped them. Not again. She would not help.

He was as alone as she was in this part of a war. His back still oozed and the wounds on his neck had become reinfected. She would get Constanza to look at the damage again and then he would be gone. It was all she could do for him.

The daughter of El Vengador sat and observed him from a distance, propped against a warm ochre wall out of the breeze. Still. Silent. Barely moving.

He almost hated her for her easy insolence and her unnamed fury. She would not help him. He knew that. She would only watch him fall again and again until he could no longer pull himself up. Then she would go and another would come to lift him back to the kapok bed in the room with its gauzy curtains, half-light and sickness.

Almost six weeks since A Coruña. Almost forty-two days since he had last eaten well. His bones looked stark and drawn against thin skin and big feet. He'd seen himself in the mirror a few days before as the man designated to tend to his needs had lifted him, eyes too large in his face, cheeks sunken.

She had stopped visiting him in his room three weeks ago, when the priest had been called to give him the last rites. He remembered the man through a fog of fever, the holy water comforting even if the sentiment lay jumbled in his mind.

'Through this holy anointing may the Lord...'

Death came on soft words and cool water. It was a part of the life of a soldier, ever present and close.

But he had not died. He had pulled himself through the heat and come out into the chill. And when he had insisted on being brought to the pathway of trees, she had come, too. Watching. Always from a distance. She would leave soon, he knew. He had fallen too many times for her to stay. His hands bled and his knee, too, caught against a root, tearing. There was no resistance left in him any more and no strength.

He hoped Daniel Wylde had got home safely. He hoped the storms he had heard about had not flung the boat his friend travelled in to the murky bottom of the Bay of Biscay. 'Jesus, help him,' he murmured. 'And let me be remembered.'

A foolish prayer. A vain prayer. His family would miss him. His mother particularly and then life would move on. New babies. Other events until he would be like the memories he carried of his father and his youngest brother, gone before their time into the shifting mists of after.

'Hell,' he swore with the first beginnings of anger. A new feeling, this. All-encompassing. Strengthening. Only wrath in it. He reached out for the fortitude and with one last push grabbed the rough bark of the scrawny olive and pulled with all his fury, up this time into a standing position, up again into the world of the living.

He did not let go, did not allow his legs to buckle, did not think of falling or failing or yielding. Nay, he held on through sharp pain and a heartbeat that raked through his ears as a drum thumping in all the parts of his body, his breath hoarse and shaking.

And then she was there with her wide green knowing eyes and her hair stuffed under the hat.

'I knew that you could do it.'

He could not help but smile.

'Tomorrow you will take more steps and the next day more again and the day after that you will walk from this path to that one. And then you will go home.'

Her face was fierce and sharp. There was blood on her sleeve and on her fingers. New blood. Fresh blood. He wondered why. She saw where he looked and lifted her chin.

'The French have taken A Coruña and Ferrol. A resounding defeat with Soult now walking the streets of the towns unfettered. Soon the whole of the north will be theirs.'

'War…has its…losers.'

'And its cowards,' she tossed back. 'Better to have not come here at all if after the smallest of fights you turn tail and leave.'

He felt the anger and pushed it down. His back ached and his vision blurred and the cold that had hounded the British force through the passes of a Cantabrian winter still hovered close.

Cowards. The word seared into vehemence. So many soldiers lost in the retreat. So much bravery discovered as they had turned their backs against the sea and fought off the might of France. All he could remember was death, blood and courage.

'You need to sit down.' These new words were softer, more generous, and in one of the few times since she had found him on the fields above A Coruña, she touched him. A hand cupped beneath his elbow and another across his back. A chain lay around her neck, dipping into the collar of her unbuttoned shirt. He wondered what lay on the end of it; the thought swept away as she angled the garden chair beneath him and helped him to sit.

His breath shook as much as his hands did when he lifted them up across his knees.

'Thank...you.' And he meant it. If she had not been behind him seeing to his balance, he knew he would have fallen and the wooden seat felt good and steady and safe. Shutting his eyes against the glare of the morning, he allowed his mind to run across his body, accepting the injury, embracing the pain. The witch doctors in Jamaica had shown him this trick once when he had taken a sickness there. He had used such mesmerising faithfully ever since.

* * *

The Englishman had gone from here some-how, his body still and his heartbeat slowing to a fraction of what it had been only a moment before. Even his skin cooled.

Uneasiness crept in. She could not under-stand who he was, what he was. A soldier. A fighter. A spy. A man who spoke both the high and low dialects of Spain as well as any native and one who knew at every turn and at every moment exactly what was happen-ing about him. Alejandra could see this in his stance as well as in his eyes now opened, the blue today paler than it had ever looked; alert and all-knowing.

She had never seen another like him. Even worn down to exhaustion she caught the quick glance he chanced behind to where a line of her father's men were coming in from the south. Gauging danger, measuring response.

'Where will I be sent…on from?' His gaze narrowed.

It was seldom she told anyone of plans that did not include the next hour, for it gave the asker too much room to wriggle free of any constraints. With him she was honest.

'Not from here. It is too dangerous in A Coruña now. You will leave from the west.'

'From one of the small ports in the Rias Altas, then?'

So Captain Lucien Howard knew his geography, but not his local politics.

'No, that area harbours too many enemies of my father. It shall not be there.' She turned and looked up at the sky, frowning. 'There is a storm coming in with the wind from the ocean.'

The clouds had amassed and darkened across the horizon, a thick band of leaden grey just above the waterline.

My father needs to find out who you are first before he lets you go. He needs to understand your people and your character and the danger you might pose to us should you not be the man you say you are. And if you are not...

These thoughts she kept to herself.

'I am not your enemy, Alejandra.' He seldom called her by her given name, but she liked it. Soft. Almost whispered. Her heart beat a little faster, surprising her, annoying her, and she looked away, making much of watching those who had come in from Betanzos. Tomeu was amongst them, shading his face and peering at them, the bandage on his wrist white in the light even at this distance.

'But neither are you my friend, Ingles, for all your sacrifice and devotion to the cause of Spain.'

He laughed, the edges of his eyes creasing, and she took in breath. What was it about him that made her more normal indifference shatter? She even imagined she might have blushed.

'I am here, *señorita*, because of a mistake.'

Now, this was new. A piece of personal information that he offered without asking.

'A mistake?'

'I spent too long in the Hercules Tower looking for the British transports. They had not arrived and the French were circling.'

'So they found you there?'

'Hardly.' This time there was nothing but cold ice in his glance. 'They had taken one of my men and I thought to save him.'

'And did you?'

'No.'

The wind could be heard above their silence. Strengthening and changing direction. Soon the sun would be gone and it would rain. The beating pulse in a vein of his throat below his left ear was the only sign of great emotion and greater fury. So very easy to miss.

'He was a spy, like you?'

He nodded. 'There are weaknesses that are found out only under great duress. Jealousy. Greed. Fear. For Guy the weakness was cowardice, but he ran in the wrong direction.'

'So you left him there? As a punishment?'

'No. I tried to bring him safely through the lines of the French. I failed.'

For some men, Alejandra thought, the rigours of war brought forward cowardice. For others it highlighted a sheer and bloody-minded bravery. She imagined what it must have cost Captain Lucien Howard in pain to try to rescue his friend. She doubted anyone or anything could push him into doing that he did not wish to, but still, most men held a limit of what was sacred and worth dying for and a well-aimed hurt usually brought results.

Her father was the master of it.

But this Englishman's strength, even in the lines of his wasted and marked body, was obvious. Unbreakable and stalwart. She imagined, given the choice, that he would choose death over dishonour and pain across betrayal.

She wondered if she could manage the same.

The blood from his torn hands stained his white shirt and the sweat from his exertions had darkened the linen.

But he was beautiful with his pale eyes and his gold hair, longer now after weeks of sickness and fallen from the leather tie he more normally sported. She wanted to run her fingers through the length of it just to see it against the dark of her own skin.

Contrasts.

Inside and out.

Lucien. The name suited him with its silky vowels. Almost the name of one of the three archangels in the Bible, the covering angel, the fallen one. Alejandra shook her head and cleared her thoughts.

'I will send Constanza to you again tonight with her herbs. She has a great prowess in the healing arts.'

When he brushed back his hair the sun flinted in the colour. 'If she leaves the ointment in my room, I can tend to it myself.'

'As you wish, then.'

Kicking at the mud beneath her feet, once and then another time, she left him to the coming rain and the wind and the rising tides of fortune, and when she reached the hacienda's stables she turned once to see the shadow of him watching her.

Chapter Three

Lucien woke in the night to a small and quiet noise. He had been trained well to know the difference in sounds and knew that the louder ones were those less likely to kill you.

This one was soft and muffled. He tensed into readiness.

The door opened and a candle flared as Alejandra's father came to sit on the small stool near the bed, stretching his long legs out before him and grimacing as though in pain.

'You sleep lightly, Capitán.'

'Years of practice, *señor*,' Lucien returned.

'Put the knife away. I am only here to talk.'

Lucien slipped the blade beneath his pillow, angling it so that it might be taken up quickly again if needed. He did not think the man opposite missed the inherent threat.

Alejandra had brought him the weapon on his second evening here, a quiet offering in the heat of his fever.

'For protection,' she had said in warning. 'I am presuming you know how to use it. If not, it is probably better...' He'd simply reached out and taken it from her, the insult smarting given the wounds on his back.

Tonight her father looked weary and he took his time in forming the message before he spoke.

'It has come to my notice that you are a peer of the English aristocracy, Capitán Howard.' The ring Lucien had been wearing lay in the older man's hand when he opened his fingers, the Ross family coat of arms shining in the candlelight. He thought it had been lost for ever. 'Lord Lucien Howard, the sixth Earl of Ross. The title sits on your shoulders as the head of your household and you wield a good deal of power in English society.'

Lucien remained silent for he was certain that there would be more to come.

'But your family seat is bankrupt by all accounts. Poor investments by your father and his father, it is said, and now there is very little in the Howard coffers. Soon there will be nothing.'

Well, that was not a secret, Lucien thought bitterly. The penury of the earldom of Ross was well known. Anyone could have told him of it.

But his attention was taken by a sheaf of papers the other man lifted into view. He saw his own face on the front cover of *The Times*, a black-and-white copy of a likeness his mother had once commissioned of him, smiling as if he meant it. My God, it seemed an age since he had done so with any sincerity.

'You have a good number of brothers and sisters and a mother who is heartbroken because you are presumed dead.'

Lucien imagined her grief. The Countess was neither a big woman nor a particularly robust one. If this killed her before he managed to get back…

'So I have a further proposition for you, my lord.' The last two words were coated with a violent dislike. 'I could slice your throat open here and now and no one would ever know what had happened to you, or…' He stopped.

El Vengador was a man who used theatrics to the full extent, Lucien thought and humoured him. 'Or…'

'Or as an earl you are well placed to offer us even more.'

Lucien closed his eyes momentarily. This guerrilla leader was a dangerous adversary and a man who would not make an easy ally. He was also holding all the cards as far as Lucien's life was concerned. Oh, granted, he knew that he might take a good handful of men with him if he were to fight his way out of here, but he was weak and he was also, to some extent, in debt to the man for his life.

But there were things that were not being said. Lucien was sure of it. He looked the other man straight on.

'Why me? Why not someone integrated into the fabric of English society, someone from here? It seems you have agents there already. Why not use them?' Lucien's eyes turned to the papers and the ring.

'But we could not access the places you do, my lord. We could never hope to be within ear-shot of a king.'

'Society and the monarch do not write the law. England has a democracy and a parliament to do that.'

'And one of the Houses of Parliament consists of peers of the realm. Your name is included in that representation, is it not, Lord Ross?'

Finally he was gathering the sense of this assignment. If he had not been titled, he would probably have been disposed of by now and this conversation was a warning of it.

El Vengador held men in London, dangerous men, men with dreams of a Spanish free land in their hearts and the means to ensure it had the best chance of fruition.

England and Spain might be on the same side of the fight against Napoleon, but each had their own reasons for victory and the milksop version of democracy held by the Spanish army and the splintered *juntas* was a very different one from that offered by the guerrilla leaders. 'The little war' was the translation, but Lucien had heard tales of the French being killed in their hundreds by the partisan bands roaming the rough and isolated passes of the northern countryside, and many of those deaths had not been a pretty sight.

'The guerrilla movement might strike terror into the hearts of the French troops, but you also frighten much of the Spanish population with your forced conscription and looting.' He refrained from adding savagery and barbarousness to the list. 'What makes you think I would want to help you? I do not wish to be the person who facilitates the death of my countrymen should a battle be badly lost and you have all the personal details of each commanding officer.'

A movement of the door had both of them turning. Alejandra came in. She had been asleep. He could see the remains of slumber in the flush on her cheeks and in the tangle of her hair.

God. She slept fully clothed and with a knife as close as his. The silver of her dagger glimmered in the candlelight. He was surprised she had not sheathed it when she saw her father in the room.

'I am not here to kill him, *hija*.'

An explanation of intention that underlined her presence. Lucien frowned. Did she sleep near? To protect him? Her eyes did not meet his own as they took in the papers and his ring sitting on the table to one side of the bed, giving him the notion that she had known of her father's quest. And of the danger.

'You will take him to the boat in a week, Alejandra. No later.'

'Very well.' Her answer held the same edge of hardness as her father's.

'Find another to travel with you. Tomeu, perhaps?'

She shook her head. 'No. I shall take Adan. He has people to the west and good contacts.'

'Then it is decided.' El Vengador's fingers drummed against his thigh as he stood. 'I do not expect you to do this work for Spain without reward, Lord Ross. A sum of money shall be deposited into a bank of your choice as soon as any business between us is conducted and I am satisfied with the intelligence.'

A *fait accompli*. Perhaps El Vengador was not used to having men turn down his offers of assistance. Still, he was in the lair of the tiger, so to speak, and it would be unwise to annoy him.

'I will think carefully on what you have proposed.'

A hand came forward, grasping his own in a surprisingly firm and warm way.

'For freedom,' the older man said as Lucien watched him. 'And victory.'

Then he was gone. Alejandra stood against the wall to the left of the window, one foot bent so that it rested against the peeling ochre. Ready to flee.

'You knew about this?' He gestured to the paper and the ring. 'You knew what your father might ask?'

'Or of what he might not,' she returned and crossed the room to stand beside him, lifting *The Times* in her hands.

'You look younger when you smile.'

'It's an old likeness.'

This time she laughed and the sound filled the room like warm honey, low and smooth.

'I think, Lord Lucien Howard, sixth Earl of Ross, that even my father could not kill you if he wanted to.'

'I hope, Alejandra, only daughter of El Vengador, that you are right.'

She placed the paper down with as much care as she had used to pick it up. No extra movements. No uncertain qualms. Death could have been in the room when she entered as easily as life and yet there was not one expression on her face that told him of either relief or disappointment.

But she had come and her knife was sheathed now, back in the soft leather at her left ankle.

Would she have fought her father for him? The thought knocked the breath from his lungs.

'Thank you.' He offered the words, no sentiment in them but truth, and by the look on her face he knew she understood exactly what such gratitude was for.

She was gone as quietly as her father had left, one moment there and the next just the breeze of her going. He heard the door close with a scrape of the latch.

He dreamt of Linden Park, the Howard seat at Tunbridge Wells, with the sun on its windows and the banks of the River Teise lined with weeping willows, soft green in the coat of early spring. His father was there and his brother. The bridge had not collapsed yet and he had not had to try to save them as they turned over and over in the cold current, dragged down by heavy clothing, late rains and panic.

His mind found other happier moments—his sister, Christine, and he as they had ridden across the surrounding valleys, as fast as the wind, the sound of starlings and wrens and the first gambolling lambs in the fields.

He thought of Daniel Wylde, too, and of

Francis St Cartmail, and them all as young boys constructing huts in the woods and hunting rabbits with his father's guns. Gabriel Hughes had come sometime later, on horseback, less talkative than the others, but interesting. Gabe had taught Lucien the trick of holding one's own counsel and understanding the hidden meaning of words that were not quite being said.

And then Alejandra was there in his thoughts, her long hair down her back and her skin lustrous in candlelight, full lips red and eyes dark. In his dream she wore a thin and flowing nightgown, the shape of her lithe body seen easily through it. He felt himself harden as the breath in him tightened. She came against him like molten fire, acquiescent and searching, her mouth across his own as her head tipped up, taking all that he offered; sweet heat and an unhidden desire before she plunged a knife deep through the naked and exposed gap in his ribs.

'Hell.' He came awake in a second, panting, shocked, his member rock solid and ready, the stupidity in him reeling. For the first time in all the weeks of pain and terror and exhaustion he felt like crying; for him and for her and for a war that held death as nothing more than a debt of sacrifice on its laboured way to victory.

Alejandra was her father's daughter. She had told him that again and again in every way that counted. In her distance and her disdain. In her sharpened blade held at the ready and the rosary she often played with, bead by bead of entreaty and Catholic confession.

Yet still the taste of her lingered in his mouth, and the feel of her flesh on his skin had him pushing back the sheets, a heat all-encompassing even in the cold of winter.

What would happen on the road west, he wondered, the thought of long nights in her company when the moon was high and shadow clothed the landscape? How many days was the journey? How many miles? If he was not to be taken out of Spain by way of the Rias Altas, was it the more southern Rias Baixas they meant to use? Or even the busy seaport of Vigo?

The dream had changed him somehow, made him both less certain and more foolish, the unreality of it sharpened by a hope he hated.

He wished there was brandy left at his bedside or some Spanish equivalent of a strong and
alcoholic brew, but there was only the water infused with oranges, honey and mint. He took
up the carafe and drank deeply, the quickened
beat of his heart finally slowing.

Reaching over to the table, he slipped the
signet ring on his finger where it had been for
all of the years of his adult life and was glad
to have it back. Then he lifted up the paper to
see the date.

February the first. His mother's birthday. He
could only guess how she had celebrated such
a milestone with this news crammed on to the
front page of the broadsheet.

He had always known it might come to this,
lost behind the enemy lines and struggling to
survive, but he had not imagined a thin and
distant girl offering him protection even as she
swore she did not. Taking his blade from beneath his pillow, he tucked it into the leather he
had found in one of the drawers in this room
before placing it back on the bedside table and
glancing at the pendulum clock on the far wall.

Almost four, the heavy tick and tock of it
filling silence. He would not sleep again.

He tried recalling the maps of Spain he had held in his saddlebag on the long road north to the sea. He and his group of guides had drawn many images, measuring the distances and topography, the ravines and the crossable passes, the rivers and the bridges and the levels of water. Much of what they transcribed he had determined himself as they had traversed across into the mountains, the margins of each impression filled with comments and personal observations.

When he had encountered the French soldiers the folder had been lost, for he had not seen it since lying wounded on the field above the town. He could probably redraw much of it from memory, but the loss of such intelligence was immense. Without knowledge of the local landscape the British army was caught in the out-of-date information that allowed only poor and dangerous passage.

A noise brought him around to the door once again and this time it was the one named Tomeu who stood watching him.

'May I speak with you, Ingles?'

Up close the man who had helped him from the battleground was younger than he remembered him to be. His right wrist was encased in a dirty bandage.

He closed the door carefully behind himself and stood there for a moment as if listening. 'I am sorry to come so late, Capitán, but I leave in an hour for the south and I wanted to catch you before I went. I saw your candle still burnt in the gap beneath the door and took the chance to see if you were awake.'

Lucien nodded and the small upwards pull of the newcomer's lips changed a sullen lad into a more handsome one.

'My name is Bartolomeu Diego y Betancourt, *señor*, and I am a friend of Alejandra's.' He waited after delivering this piece of news, eyes alert.

'I recognise you. You are the one who got me on the canvas stretcher behind the horse the morning after I was hurt.'

'I did not wish to. I thought you would have been better off dead. It was Alejandra who insisted we bring you here. If it had been left to me, I would have plunged my blade straight through your heart and finished it.'

'I see.'

'Do you, *señor*? Do you really understand

how unsafe it is for Alejandra at the hacienda now that you are here and what your rescue might have cost her? El Vengador has his own demons and he is ruthless if anyone at all gets in his way.'

'Even his daughter?'

That brought forth a torrent of swearing in Spanish, a bawdy long-winded curse. 'Enrique Fernandez will end his life here in bitterness and hate. And if Alejandra stays with him, so will she, for her stubbornness is as strong as his own. Fernandez has enemies who will pounce when he is least expecting it and a host of others who are jealous of his power.'

'Like you?'

The young man turned away.

'She said you were clever and that you could see into thoughts that should remain private. She said you were more dangerous than even her father and that if you stay here much longer, El Vengador would know it to be such and have you murdered.'

'Alejandra said this?'

'Yes. She wants you gone.'

'I know.'

'But she wants you safe, too.'

He stayed quiet as Tomeu went on.

'She is like a sister to me. If you ever hurt her...'

'I will not.'

'I believe you, Capitán, and that is one of the reasons I am here. You, too, are powerful in your own right, powerful enough to protect her, perhaps?'

'You think Alejandra would accept my protection?' He might have laughed out loud if the other man had not looked both so very serious and so very young.

'Her husband was killed less than one year ago, a matter of months after their marriage.'

'I see.' And Lucien did. It was the personal losses that made a man or a woman fervent and Alejandra was certainly that.

'Are there other relatives?'

'An uncle down south somewhere, but they are not close.'

'Friends, then, apart from you?'

'This is a fighting unit, ranging across this northern part of Spain with the express purpose of causing chaos and mayhem. Most of the women are gone either to safety or to God. It is a dangerous place to inhabit.'

'Here today and gone tomorrow?'

'Exactly.'

'Was it Alejandra who hurt your wrist?'

'It was. I asked her to be my wife and she refused.'

Lucien smiled. 'A comprehensive no, then.'

'The bruise on her face was an accident. I dragged her down the stairs with me after losing my footing. She said she would never marry anyone again and even the asking of it was an insult. To her. She never listens, you see, never takes the time to understand her own and ever-present danger.'

'She loved her husband, then?'

The other man laughed. 'You will need to ask her that, *señor.*'

'I will. So you think her father would harm her?'

'El Vengador? Not intentionally. But your presence here is difficult for them both. Alejandra wants you well enough to travel, but Enrique only wants you gone. The title you hold has swung opinion in your favour a little, but with the slightest of pushes it could go the other way and split us all asunder. Better not to care too much about the health and welfare of others in this compound, I think. Better, too, to have you bundled up and heading for home.'

A safer topic, this one. But every word that Tomeu had spoken told Lucien something of his authority. A man like El Vengador would not be generous in his fact sharing, yet this young man had a good knowledge of the conversation he had just had with Alejandra's father. Lucien had seen him glance at the signet ring back on his finger and in the slight flare of his eyes he had understood just what Tomeu did not say.

He was a lieutenant perhaps, or at least one who participated in the decision-making for the group. The young face full of smiles and politeness almost certainly masking danger, for the lifeblood of the guerrilla movement was brutality and menace.

Had Alejandra's father sent Tomeu to sound him out? Had Alejandra herself? Or was this simply a visit born from expediency and warning?

Thirty-two years of living had made Lucien question everything and in doing so he was still alive.

'What of her groom's family? Could she go there to safety?'

'My cousin, *señor*, and they want the blood of the Fernandez family more than anyone else in Spain. More than the French, even, and that is saying something.'

This was what war did.

It tore apart the fabric and bindings of society and replaced them with nothing. He thought of his own immediate family in England and then of his large extended one of aunts, uncles and cousins. Napoleon and the French had a lot to answer for the wreckage that was the new Europe. He suddenly wished he was home.

'I am sorry...' Lucien left the words dangling. Sorry for them all. It was no answer, he knew, but he could promise nothing else. As if the young man understood, he, too, turned for the door.

'Do not trust anyone on your trip to the west.'

'I won't.'

'And watch over Alejandra.'

With that he was gone, out into the fading night of a new-coming dawn, for already Lucien could hear the first chorus of birdsong in the misty air.

Chapter Four

The anger in Alejandra was a red stream of wrath, filling her body from head to foot, making her hot and cold and sick.

Tomeu had left, travelling south into more danger, and the Englishman was in his usual place on the pathway between the olive trees, struggling to walk.

Up and down. Slowly. He was not content with a small time of it, either, but had been there for most of the morning, sweat everywhere despite the cold of the day.

He was getting better, that much she could tell. He did not limp any more or lean over his injuries like a snail in a shell, cradling his hurt. No, straight as any soldier, he picked his way from this tree to that one and then back again, using the seat on every third foray now to stop and find breath.

Stubborn.

Like her.

She smiled at that thought and the tension released a little. She knew he must have his knife upon him for she had been into his room whilst he was out there and checked; a poor choice that, an act of thieves and sneaks. It was who she had become here, in this war of Spain. Her mother would have castigated her severely for such a lapse of decorum, but now no one cared. She had become part of the campaign to please her father, dressing as a boy and assembling intelligence because he was all she had left of family.

Lucien Howard suddenly saw her for he raised his hand in greeting. So very English. Someone like him, no doubt, would keep his manners intact even upon his deathbed. It was why his country did so well in the world, she reasoned, this conduct of decency and rectitude even in the face of extreme provocation.

'I had a visit from your friend Tomeu last night.'

Shocked, she could only stare at him.

'Well, that answers my first question,' he returned and sat down. 'I thought you might have known.'

'What did he say?' A thousand things ran around in her head, things that she sincerely hoped he had not told this Englishman.

'That you were married to his cousin. For a month.'

'A short relationship,' she gave back, hating the way her voice shook with the saying of it.

'Tomeu also confided that he himself had asked you to be his wife, but you had refused.'

All of the secrets that were better hidden. 'He was talkative, then.'

'Unlike you. He implied you were in danger here.'

At that she laughed. 'Implied? It surrounds us, Capitán. Three hundred thousand enemy troops with their bloodthirsty generals and an emperor who easily rules Europe.'

'I think he might have meant danger on a more personal level.'

'To me?'

When he nodded she knew exactly what Tomeu had said, for he had used the same arguments on her when she had broken his wrist.

'He talks too much and I did not ask for your help. It was you who needed mine.'

He ignored that sarcasm. 'He said the trip west might be difficult. The power your father holds has aggravated those who would take it from him, it seems. Including Tomeu.'

At that she smiled. 'When my father asks you again to aid the effort for Spanish independence, say yes, even if you have no intention of doing so.'

'Because he will kill me if I don't?'

'He is a man with little time to accomplish all he feels he must. To him you are either the means to an end or the end. Your life depends on how much honour you accord to your word, Capitán. My advice would be to allot it none.'

'A promise here means nothing?'

'Less than nothing. Integrity is one of the first casualties of war.' Alejandra held her mouth in the grim edge of a scowl she had become so good at affecting and did not waver. She was pleased when he nodded.

'When your mother was alive…'

She did not let him finish.

'We will leave here in a few days and head west. There will be two others who travel with us and my father will provide you with a warm coat and sturdy boots.'

His own were cracking at the soles, she thought, the poorly made footwear of the English army was a disgrace. What manufacturer would cut corners for profit when the lives of its fighting men were at stake?

Honour. The word slid into the space between them like a serpent, pulled this way and then that, unravelled by pragmatism and greed.

'We will travel into the mountains first, so you will need to have the strength to climb.' Despite meaning not to, her eyes glanced around at the flat small space that lay between the olives. Hardly the foothills of the mountains. The questionable wisdom of her plan made her take in a breath.

She did not want Captain Lucien Howard to die in the wastes of the alpine scrub, made stiff by ice and cold by rain. She could help him a little, but with Adan and Manolo tagging along she understood they would not countenance anything that endangered safety.

He would have to manage or he would die.

She knew he saw that thought in her eyes because he suddenly smiled.

Beautiful. Like the picture in his English newspaper, the sides of his mouth and eyes creasing into humour. She wished he had been ugly or old or scarred. But he was not. He was all sapped strength, wasted brawn and outrageous beauty. And cleverness. That was the worst of it, she suddenly thought, a man who might work out the thoughts and motivations of others and set it to work for his advantage.

'I will be fit for the journey. Already I feel stronger.'

When he leant forward Alejandra saw the bandage at his neck had slipped and the redraw skin was exposed. It would scar badly, a permanent reminder of this place and this time.

Lucien knew Alejandra worried about the wound on his neck, though she smoothed her face in that particular habit she had so that all thoughts were masked.

He imagined getting home to the safe and unscathed world of the *ton*, with war written on him beneath superfine wool. The hidden history on his back in skin and sinew would need to be concealed from all those about him, for who would be able to understand the cost of it and how many would pity him?

A further distance. Another layer. Sometimes he felt he was building them up like children's blocks, the balance of who he was left in danger of tipping completely.

Except here with Alejandra in the light of a Spanish winter morning, the grey-green of olive branches sending dappled shadows across them.

Here he did not have to pretend who he was or wasn't and he was glad.

Without her watching from a distance he might not have found the mental strength to try again and again and again to get up and move when everything ached and stung and hurt. She challenged him and egged him on. No sorrow in it or compassion. Both would have broken him.

Breathing out, he rose from the seat and stood. He was always surprised just how much taller he was than her.

'Tomorrow I will walk to the house.'

'It is more than two hundred yards away, *señor*,' she said back, the flat tone desultory.

'And back,' he continued and smiled.

Unexpectedly she did, too, green eyes dancing with humour and the dimples in both cheeks deep.

He imagined her in a ballroom in London, hair dressed and well-clothed. Red, he thought. The colour of her gown would need to be bold. She would be unmatched.

'If you walk that far, Ingles, I will bring you a bottle of the best *aguardiente de orujo*.'

'Firewater?' he returned. 'I have heard of this but have not tried it.'

'Drink too much and the next day you will be in bed till the sundown, especially if you are not used to the strength of it. But drink just enough and the power fills you.'

'Would you join me in the celebration?'

She tipped her head up and looked him straight in the eyes. 'Perhaps.'

Lucien spent the evening on the floor of his room exercising and trying to get some strength into his upper body. He could feel the muscles remembering what they had once been like, but he was a couple of stone lighter with his sickness and the shaking that overtook him after heavy exertion was more than frustrating.

So he lay there on the polished tiled floor and watched the ceiling whilst his heart rate slowed and the anger cooled. Just two months ago he could have so easily managed all that he now could not.

He cleared his mind and imagined the walk from the trees to the outhouse and back. He'd walk past the first olive tree and then on to the sheltered path with lavender on each edge. The hedges were clipped there and could not be used for balance and after that there were three steps that came up to the covered porch. Two hundred yards there and another two hundred back and flat save for the stairs.

Of course he could manage such a distance. He only had to believe it.

The marks drawn into the plaster beneath the windows caught his attention again. Closer up he could see they formed a pattern different from the one he had first thought.

There were many more indents than he had originally imagined, smaller scrawlings caught in between the larger strokes. Twenty-nine. Thirty-one. Fifteen. Days of the months, perhaps? His mind quickly ran across the year. February and March was a sequence that worked and 1808 had been a leap year. But why would anybody keep such a track of time?

A noise through the inside wall then also caught his attention, quiet and muffled. Plainly it was the sound of someone crying and he knew without a doubt that it was Alejandra. Her room was next to his, the thickness of a stone block away.

Rising, he stood and tipped his head to the stone. One moment turned into two and then there was silence. It was as if on the other side of the wall she knew he was there, too, listening and knowing. He barely allowed himself breath.

She could feel him there, a foot away through the plaster and stone, knew that he stood where she had stood for all of the months at the end of Juan's life; he a prisoner of her father's, a man who had betrayed the cause.

She could not save Captain Lucien Howard should Papa decide that he was expendable, so she needed to take him out of here to the west. The evening light drew in on itself, watchful, the last bird calls and then the quiet. Juan had lost his speech and his left arm, but he had lingered for two of the months of winter and into the first weeks of spring. She had prayed each day that it would be the end and marked the wall when it was not.

Her marks were still there, the indents of time drawn into the plaster, one next to the other near the base of the wall, and left there when he passed away as a message and a warning.

Betray El Vengador and no one is safe, not even the one married to his only daughter. Juan had died with a rosary in his hands. Her father had, at least, allowed him that.

A year ago now, before the worst of the war. She wondered how many more men would be gone by the same time next year and, crossing her room, took out the maps of the northern mountains that Lucien Howard had upon him when he was captured. Precise and detailed. With such drawings the passage through the Cantabrians for a marauding army would be an easy thing to follow. She wondered why the French had not thought to search his saddlebags and take the treasure after leaving him for dead on the field.

Probably the rush of war had allowed the

mistake. Not torture, but battle. Certainly the swords drawn against the Englishman had not been carefully administered, but made in the hurried flurry of panic.

She ought to deliver these maps into the hands of her father, but something stopped her. Papa did not need information to make his killings easier, no matter what she thought of the French. These were English maps, any military advantage gained belonged to them. On the road west she would give them back to the captain to take home and say nothing of them to her father. Perhaps they might be some recompense for Lucien Howard coming into Spain with an army that had been far too small and an apology, too, for his substantial injuries.

She felt tired out from her worrying, shattered by her father's reactions to the Englishman. She had hardly slept in weeks for the dread of finding him with his throat cut or simply not there when she hovered outside his chamber just to see that he still breathed.

She did not want to be this person, this worrier. But no matter how the day started and how many hours she could stretch it out between making sure he was neither dead nor gone, she also couldn't truly relax until the continued health and welfare of Captain Lucien Howard had been established.

A knock on the door had her standing very still and she glanced at herself in the mirror opposite. She looked as if she had been crying, her eyes red and swollen. The knock came again.

'Who is it?' Her tone was strong.

'Your father, Alejandra. Can I come in?'

Concealing the maps in a drawer, she wiped at her eyes with the sleeve of her jacket and rubbed her cheeks. If the skin there was a little redder, her eyes would not show up quite so much. Then she flicked the lock.

Enrique Fernandez y Castro strode in and shut the door behind him. Slowly. She knew the exact second he recognised she had been upset.

'If your mother were here…' he began, but she shook that train of thought away and he remained silent.

Rosalie Santo Domingo y Giminez stood between them in memory and sometimes this was the only thing they still had in common, their love for a woman who had been good and brave and was gone. Both of them had dealt with her death in different ways, her father with his anger and his wars and her with a sense of distance that sometimes threatened to overcome her completely. But they seldom spoke of Rosalie now. To lessen the anguish, she surmised, and to try to survive life with the centre of their world missing.

'The English earl is gaining his strength back.' This was not phrased as a question. 'I have heard he is a man of intellect and intuition. What do you make of him?'

'A good man, I think, Papa. A man who might do your bidding in London well if you let him.'

'He could be dangerous. To you on the way west. Others could take him.'

Alejandra knew enough of her father to feign indifference, for if she insisted on accompanying Lucien Howard she also knew that he would surely change his plans, so she stayed silent.

'Tomeu says he can read minds.'

At that she laughed. 'And you believe him?'

'I believe there might be more to him than we can imagine, Alejandra, and we need to take care that he knows only so much about us.'

'The house, you mean. The security of this place and the manpower?'

'Take him out blindfolded. I do not wish for him to see the gates or the bridges. Or the huts down by the river.'

'Very well.'

'And leave him in Corcubion, no further. You should be able to find him a boat to England from there and it is a lot closer.'

'Adan has family in Pontevedra.'

'Almost a week away by the mountain paths. I want you back sooner.'

'Very well.' Her mind reeled with the implications of sending him from a town that did not have the protections of the others.

'Here is a purse.' The leather bag was tied with plaited rope and it was heavy. 'He costs me much, this British spy. If you feel at any time he is not worth the danger, then kill him. I have instructed Adan and Manolo to do the same. Anything at all that might bring trouble. You will leave here three days from now.'

'But he is not well enough, Papa.'

'If he can't walk out of here by then, he will never do anything else. Do you understand me, daughter? No more.'

'Indeed.' Her father wanted the English captive gone and if it could not be done with any sense of decorum, then he would simply get rid of the problem altogether. 'But we will leave when it is dark for it will be safer that way.' She needed to give Captain Howard time to acclimatise and the night-time would help. If they went late, it would mean only a few hours of walking.

'Good. I shall not see him before he goes for I am off to Betanzos before dawn on the morrow and will be there for a week. Give him my promise that someone will be contacting him. Soon.'

'I shall.'

He smiled at that, a quiet movement that made him look more like the handsome and kind father of old. It seemed so long since she had felt such kinship.

'Go with God, Alejandra.' He tipped his head and left the room, the sound of his steps on the tiles outside fading.

She had three days to prepare the English captain for the gruelling walk, though now they would not go into the mountains, it seemed, but along the coast. That might be easier for him, but harder for them with the lack of cover. Juan's family, the Diego y Betancourts, inhabited this part of the land and they would need to take care to avoid notice.

Swearing softly, she thought of the difficult steps the captain had managed today. No more than a few hundred hard-fought yards till he needed to rest.

In three days he would not have that luxury. Extracting her rosary from her top pocket, she prayed to the Lord for strength, courage and perseverance. For both of them.

Lucien took in breath.

The new day was cloudless but cold and Alejandra stood beside him watching. Further afield he saw a group of others turn and stare.

'Don't come with me,' he instructed as she took the first step when he did. 'Wait here and I will be back.'

'The *orujo* will warm you, *señor.*' No 'good luck' or whispered encouragement. He was glad for it.

He was neither dizzy today nor light-headed and he had eaten a substantial breakfast for the first time in weeks. He was also aware of the heavy shadows beneath Alejandra's eyes.

Taking the first step, he kept on going. The hedges of lavender were at each side of him now, he could smell the scent of the leaves, heady and pungent. Then the small space of chipped stones and the three rising steps.

He stopped before them and redrew in breath. He was sweating and the bravado that he had started with had waned a little, the stairway requiring a lot more in effort than the flatness of the path.

There was no handrail, nothing to hold on to as he raised one foot and transferred his weight. One. Two. Three. The deck welcomed him and shaded him, another flower he had no notion of sending a pungent odour into the air all around.

When he turned he saw her, standing still against the olives in the distance, her hands knotted before her as if she had been certain he might fall.

He smiled and she smiled back, the journey now easier in its return.

He could do it, the steps, the pathway, the lavender hedges and then back to the trees where he had left her. He did not even need to sit down when he reached the olives, but stood there, snatching the hat from his head and taking the ornate glass cup that she had filled from her hand.

'*Salud.*'

'Good health,' Lucien gave back in English and their beakers touched, the cold of the tipple drawing trails across glass. He was elated with his progress and far less exhausted than he imagined he might have been. Tomorrow he would try for a longer distance and the next day more again.

'We leave in two nights for the west.'

That soon? The liquor burnt down his throat and touched the nausea that roiled in his stomach, but he would not let her see that as he took another sip.

Despite his success this morning he could not even imagine climbing into the foothills of the Cantabrians or the Galicians and pretending energy and health for hours and hours on end.

'If you lag behind, you will be shot. My father's orders.'

Finishing his drink, he held out his glass for more. 'Then I hope the firewater is all that you say it is.'

'Papa has enemies here and the French have

not withdrawn. But we know this place like the back of our hands, the secret trails, the hidden paths, and we will be armed.'

'We?'

'Adan, Manolo and I.' She looked around as if to check no one else was close. 'You have your knife, Capitán. Make certain it is within easy reach and keep it hidden. If anyone threatens you, use it.'

'Anyone?' His eyes scanned her dark ones.

'Anyone at all,' she returned and finished the last of her *orujo*.

'Clothes will be brought to your room for the journey. And hair dye. The pale of your hair would give you away completely. Constanza will come and do it.'

'A disguise, then?'

He saw how she hesitated, the stories of men captured without their uniform and hanged perfunctorily so much a part of folklore. With a cloak over blue and white he might be safer, but those travelling with him would not.

'You speak Spanish like a native of this part. It will have to be enough.'

'Do you expect trouble?'

She only laughed.

The pleasure of completing the walk had receded a little, but Lucien did not want her to see it. Even the *orujo* was warring against his stomach, a strong dram that scoured his digestive system after six weeks of bland gruel.

'Can I ask you a question, Alejandra?' She nodded. 'What happened to your husband?'

The deep green of her eyes sharpened, bruising in memory. 'He betrayed us, so he died.'

The shock of her answer left him reeling. 'How?'

'The betrayal or the death?'

'Both.'

'It was almost a year ago now and it was winter and cold. There was a fight and my husband lost. He died slowly, though.'

'Three months' worth of slowly? It is his room I am in.'

'How could you possibly know that?' She had stepped back now and her voice shook.

'The marks on my wall. February had twenty-nine days in the last year only and March has thirty-one. I am presuming he died on April the fifteenth. I think you placed the marks there. To remember.'

'I did.' This time she held nothing back in

the quiet fury. 'I drew them into the plaster every night I stood in his room and wished him dead. It was for money he betrayed us. Did you figure that out, too? For the princely sum of pesos and guns, enough to start his own army and replace my father. And me.'

'He confessed?'

'No. A shot through the head was not conducive to any sort of explanation. Papa only let him live so that he might understand his reasoning and to see who else was implicated in the plot.'

'Did El Vengador find others?'

'He died without speaking again.' Her answer came back with fierceness and Lucien could see in her eyes the truth of hurt. 'Though it seems he could still write. I had not known that.'

A minute later she was gone.

The words in the Bible had been her late husband's handiwork, then? Lucien wondered what he had done to Alejandra to make her hate him so very much.

Chapter Five

Sometimes the weather in Spain, even in winter, could be windless and dry.

But on this night, early in the first week of March, the gales howled from the north in a single blowing force, enough pressure in it to make Lucien lean forward to find balance. The rains came behind, drenching, icy and cold.

His clothes at least were keeping the wet out and the warmth in. He was surprised how comfortable his new boots were and pleased the hat he had been given had a wide and angled brim. He had long since lost the feeling in his bare fingers, though.

They had been walking for a good two hours and he'd managed to keep up. Just. Alejandra hovered behind him, Adan and the other man, Manolo, cutting through the bushes ahead.

'We will stop soon.' Her words were muffled by the rain.

'And make camp?'

'More like sleep,' she returned. 'It is too dangerous to risk a fire, but the trees there will allow us at least shelter.'

He looked up. A moon was caught behind the heavy cloud, but he could see the dark shape of a line of pines about a quarter of a mile away.

He was glad for it, for although he carried very little in the bag on his back, his body ached with the prolonged exercise after such a sickness. He had not eaten much, either, his stomach still recovering from the effects of the *orujo*.

He knew Alejandra had slowed to match his pace and was thankful for it, the blunt warning she had given him still present.

Adan suddenly tipped his head. Alarmed, Lucien did the same and the sound of far-off voices came on the wind. A group of men, he determined, and ones who thought they were alone in these passes. A hand gesture had him dropping down and Alejandra crawled up beside him.

'They are about a quarter of a mile away, but heading north. Nine or ten of them, I think, with horses.'

She pulled the brown coat she wore across her head and dug into the cavity of dirt on the edge of their track.

Further ahead there was no sign at all of the others. He guessed they, too, had blended in with the undergrowth, staying put as the foreign party passed.

His eyes went to the leaves above them. Downwind. If there were dogs, they would stay safe.

Alejandra held her pistol out and her knife lay in her lap. He removed his own blade and fitted it into his fist, wishing he had been given a gun as well and rueing the loss of the fine weapons he had marched up to A Coruña with.

The rain had lightened now, beads of it across Alejandra's cheeks and in the long dark strands of hair that had escaped from the fastening beneath her hat.

He wondered if she had killed before. The faces of the many men he had consigned to the afterlife rose up in memory, numerous ghostly spectres wrapped about the heart of battle. He had long since ceased to mourn them.

The enforced rest had allowed his heartbeat to slow and the breath in him to return. Even the tiredness was held temporarily at bay by this new alertness. They were not French, he was sure of that; too few and too knowledge-able of the pathway through the foothills. A band of men of the same ilk as El Vengador, then? Guerrillas roaming the countryside. He could hear a few words of Spanish in the wind.

'It's the Belasio family,' Alejandra explained as he looked up. 'On their way back to their lands.'

'You saw them?'

She smiled and shook her head. 'I smelt them.' When her nose sniffed the air he smiled, for the rain and wind had left only wetness across the scent of winter and earth and she was teasing. Still, the small humour in the mid-dle of danger was comforting.

'They are armed partisans, too?'

'Yes.'

'Then surely we would hardly be enemies?'

'There are no hard and fast rules to this kind

of warfare. We have guns they want and your presence here would have been noted.'

'Me?'

'There is money in the exchange of prisoners. Good money, too, and it is difficult to hide the blue of your eyes. You do not look Spanish even though you speak the language well.'

He swore. 'Where are we going?'

'Corcubion. It is a small harbour two days away.'

'I thought I had heard Muros?'

She shook her head and stood. 'My father and Adan are insistent on the closer port given your condition. Come, the Belasios are gone now and the trees are not far.'

Thirty minutes later they stopped beneath the pines. It was full dark and the rain had gone, though the intermittent drips from drenched boughs above were heavy.

'We will leave again at first light.' Adan, the older of the two men, stated this as he bedded down in the lee of a medium-sized bush and the other man joined him. A good twenty yards away Alejandra stayed at Lucien's side.

He knew there was bread in his bag and he

pulled out the crust of it and began to eat. Any sustenance would see him through the next day and he needed all the energy he could muster. He wished he still had his silver flask filled with good English brandy, but it had gone with the rest of his things. The French, probably, when they had first caught him.

He did have a skin of Spanish red wine and he drank this thankfully. Alejandra simply sat there, neither eating nor drinking. She looked tired through the gloom and he handed her the skin.

Surprisingly she took it, wiping the mouth of the vessel with her sleeve when she had finished before giving it back.

'Do you want bread, too?'

She shook her head and arranged her bag as a pillow, fastening the cloak she wore about her and curling into sleep.

Overhead a bird called once. He had heard very few on the march up with the British in the lower valleys of the Cantabrians. But outside Lugo he had shot a substantial owl and sucked the warm blood from its body, because there was neither wood nor safety to cook it and he had not eaten for three days. Then he had plucked the breast and stuffed the feathers in his ruined boots to try to ward off frostbite.

He breathed out. Hard. It was relatively warm here under the trees and he had food, drink and a soft bed. The pine needles formed a sort of mattress as he lay down on his back and looked up. His knife he placed within easy reach, just outside the folds of his jacket.

'You are a careful man.' Alejandra's words were whispered.

'I have learnt that it pays to expect trouble.'

'It is my opinion that we will be safe tonight. The noise of the eagle owl, the birds you heard cry out before, is why we stop here. They roost in the trees above and are like sentries. If anything moves within a thousand yards of us, they will all be silent.'

'A comforting warning,' he returned softly, and her white teeth flashed in the darkness.

'Spain is like a lover, Señor Howard, known and giving to those who are born here. The bird sounds, the berries, the many streams and the pine needles beneath us. It is the strangers that come who change the balance of the place, the ones with greed in their eyes and the want of power.'

She saw the way he stretched out, his knife close and a sense of alertness that even sickness and a long walk had not dimmed.

She knew it had been hard for him, this climb. She had seen it in the gritted lines of his face and in the heavy beat of his pulse. His silence had told her of it, as well. It was as if every single bit of his will was used in putting one foot in front of the other and trudging on. The wine might dim the pain a little. She hoped it would.

He had removed his hat just before the light had fallen and the newly dyed darkness of his hair changed the colour of his eyes to a brighter blue. If anyone at all looked at him closely, they would know him as a stranger, a foreigner, a man to be watched.

'It is mostly downhill tomorrow.' The words came even as she meant not to say them, but there was some poignancy in one who had been so very sick and whose strength was held only by the threads of pure and utter will. He would not complain and she was thankful for it.

On her part all she wanted to do was sleep.

His presence at the hacienda had left her fretting for his safety, mindful of her father's propensity to do away with problems and so for many nights she had barely slumbered.

Here at least Manolo and Adan were a good way off and Lucien Howard's knife was sharp. There was some ease in being next to him as well and she had made sure to place her blanket roll between the captain and the others. It was as much as she could do.

The birds above called and insects buzzed about them, zinging in the night. The music of a quiet forest unthreatened by advancing armies or groups of the enemy.

She felt the warmth of Lucien Howard's shoulder as she turned away and slept.

Lucien woke as the first chorus of general birdsong sounded. Alejandra was still asleep, her arm across his as if the warmth had brought it there in a mind all of its own. One finger was badly scarred and another had lost a nail altogether. The hand of a girl who had seen hardship and pain. The lines he had noticed before on her right wrist showed up as multiple white slashes in the dullness.

He remembered all the other hands of the women of the *ton* with their painted nails and smoothness and he wanted to reach out and take her fingers in his own with a desperateness that surprised him. In sleep she looked younger, the tip tilt of her nose strangely innocent and freckles on the velvet of her cheeks.

A wood nymph and a warrior. When a spider crawled up the run of her arm he carefully brushed it away. Still, she came awake on the tiniest of touches, from slumber to complete wakefulness in less than a blink.

'Good morning.'

She did not answer him as she sat, her hair falling in a long tousled curtain to her waist, the darkness in it threaded with deeper reds and black.

He saw her glance at the sky. Determining time, he supposed, and marking the hour of dawn. The steel in her knife's hilt had left deepened ridges on the skin of her forearm, so close had she held it as she slept. When her glance took in the empty clearing she looked around.

'Where are the others?'

'They went to the stream we can hear running, about ten minutes ago. I should imagine they will be back soon.'

Standing she packed her things away and kicked at the pine needles with her feet.

'It is better no one knows we were here. A good tracker could tell, of course, but someone merely passing by...' She left the rest unsaid, but the green in her eyes was wary as she turned to him. 'Spain is not a soft country, Capitán Howard. It is a land with its heart ripped out.'

'Yet you stay here. You do not leave.'

'It's home,' she said simply and handed him a hard cooked biscuit, the top of which was brushed in a sugar syrup. 'For walking,' she explained when he looked at it without much appetite. 'If you do not eat, you will be slower.'

He felt better now that it was morning, the old sense of energy and purpose returning; perhaps it was the change of scenery or the hope of getting back to England soon that did it. His companion's smile was also a part of the equation. Without the scowl or the anger Alejandra Fernandez y Santo Domingo was beautiful. Breathtakingly so, he supposed, if she were to be seen in a gown that fitted and a face that was not always filthy.

Where the hell was this train of thought going? He pulled his mind back to their more immediate problems.

'Do you have any idea on the movements of the French?'

'Marshal Soult has taken Oporto and Marshal Victor and Joseph Bonaparte hold the centre and Madrid. They seldom travel in small groups in this part of the country anyway.'

'Because they are afraid of being picked off by the guerrillas?'

'Would you not be, too, Capitán?'

Their travelling companions were back now and Alejandra gestured to them to give her a moment as she disappeared into the bushes in the direction of the stream. Left alone with the two men, Lucien was suddenly tense. Something was wrong; he felt it in his bones and he was too much of a soldier not to take notice. He had his knife out instantly as he turned to find the threat.

'Someone's close,' he said, 'to the east.' Manolo and Adan also drew their weapons and moved up beside him.

They came out of nowhere, a group of men dressed in a similar fashion as they were, the first discharging gun slamming straight into the gut of Adan. He fell like a stone, dead as he hit the ground, eyes wide to the heavens above in surprise. Lucien had his knife at the assailant's throat before the man could powder up again, slicing the artery in a quick and simple task of death. Then he did the same to the next one. Alejandra was in the clearing now, her knife out and her breathing loud. He stepped in front of her, keeping her out of the line of fire. Two more men, he counted. Manolo disposed of one and then fell against flashing steel. As Lucien advanced the last man simply turned tail and ran. Stooping to pick up a stone, he threw it as hard as he could and was pleased to hear a yelp further away. He'd have liked to have sent his blade, too, but he did not want to lose it.

The quiet returned as quickly as it had left, the shock in Alejandra's voice vibrating as she kneeled first beside Adan and then Manolo.

'Dios mio. Dios mio. Dios mio.'

Manolo clutched her hand and tried to say something, but the words were shallow and indistinct. In return she simply held his fingers stained in blood and dirt and waited until the final breath was wrenched from him. Folding his arms across his stomach and closing his eyes, she swore roundly and stood to see to Adan. With him she arranged the cloth of his jacket across the oozing wound at his stomach before covering his eyes with her handkerchief. The small piece of fabric was embroidered with purple and blue flowers, Lucien saw, a delicate example of fine stitchery from her past.

'It was the Betancourts. I recognised them from before, but we will revenge them. It is what my father is good at.'

With a deft movement she collected the discarded weapons and water bottles and covered the bodies of her fellow partisans with pine needles, reciting some sort of prayer over them with her rosary. Then she indicated a direction. He could see tears on her cheeks, though she brushed them away with the coarse fabric of her jacket as she noticed his observation.

'We have no time to bury them properly. Those who did this will be back as soon as the others are informed and they will be baying for revenge. Adan and Manolo would not wish to die for nothing, so now we will have to use the mountain tracks to go west and see you safe.'

She struck out inland, away from the sea, the breeze behind them. As they traversed along a river, making sure to place their feet only in the rocky centre of it for a good quarter of a mile, they saw the first scree slopes of the mountains.

She listened, too, every three or four minutes stopping and turning her head into the wind so that sounds might pass down to her, in warning.

Lucien knew inside that no one followed them. Always when he had tracked for Moore across the front of a moving army he had held the knowledge of others. Here, the desolate cold and open quiet contained only safety.

The Betancourts might try to follow them, but he and Alejandra had been careful to leave no trace of themselves as they had walked and the rains had begun again, the water washing away footfalls.

'You have done this before?' he finally asked when Alejandra indicated a stop.

'As many times as you have, Capitán. Who taught you to fight with a knife like that?'

'A rum maker in Kingston Town. I was a young green officer with all the arrogance associated with it. A man by the name of Sheldon Williams took the shine off such cockiness by challenging me to a fight.'

When he saw she was interested he continued.

'It was hot, too, mid-July and no breeze, the greasy smell of the sea in the air and a good number of ships in. He could have killed me twenty times or more, but he didn't. Instead he showed me how to live.'

'You fight like my father.'

'Is that a compliment?'

She shook away his question with a frown.

She couldn't take him home now, not with Manolo and Adan dead and a father who would place the blame on the Englishman's presence for it and kill him. The horror of their deaths hit her anew as a great wave of grief broke inside.

No. She would have to take him on over the Galician Mountains and down into Pontevedra in the hope that Adan's family might help them. A longer walk and one she had done only a few times before and always under guidance.

Her whole body ached with the grief of more death, so senseless and quick.

She was on edge, too. The way Lucien Howard had slit the throats of those who had attacked them was so gracefully brutal and deceptively practised that she was wary. A man like this would make a dangerous enemy and alone with him she would need to be careful.

Still, she could not just leave him. Another thought occurred. He wore the sickness of exhaustion on his face and she noticed blood seeping again through the fabric of his jacket. From the wound on his neck, she supposed, the one that had not yet healed.

An Englishman alone in Spain would have no chance of escaping through any of the harbours on the east side of A Coruña. People here would be naturally suspicious, the scourge of the French having left a residual hatred for anyone new and different.

He spoke the language well, she would give him that, but his eyes were the light blue of a foreigner and the dye in his hair was already weakening. When she noticed the pale gold in the roots of his parting that small false truth of him firmed up resolve.

Rifling in her bag, she drew out the maps she had found concealed under the last blanket of his dead horse.

'These are yours.'

He wiped his hands against his jacket before he reached out and took the offered documents, spreading the pages wide to ascertain they were all there.

'I thought them lost.' Puzzlement lay on his brow.

'They were trapped beneath your horse and I saw them as we lifted it off you. Did you draw them?'

'Partly. I had a group of guides and the information was collated over several months of travel. Maps like this have enormous value.'

'To those who would pillage Spain? The secrets of the mountains exposed to those who would want to rape it more quickly.'

'Or protect it.'

She laughed then because she could not help it. Once, she might have believed in the noble pursuits of soldiers. 'Good or bad? There is a fine line between each, Capitán. People die here because of armies. Innocent people, and a land in winter has a limit on the succour it can

manage to harvest before starvation settles in.
In the north we have reached that limit. Another season of battle and there will be nothing
left in Galicia save for the freedom to starve.'

She had not meant to say as much, to give
a man as clever as the one before her the true
slant of her opinion. But she had ceased many
months ago to believe in the easy spoils of war
or the glory in it.

'Liberty and safety always come at a price,
I'll give you that.' His eyes were threaded with
weariness.

'And today Adan and Manolo paid for it
dearly. The French will come and then they
will go because there is no way they can stay
here and live and people like the Betancourts
will be swallowed up by bitterness and hate
until there is nothing left of them, either. That,
Capitán, is the true cost of valour. No one ever
wins. Not for ever. Not even for a little while.'

'But is not simply accepting subjugation the
true meaning of surrender?' The planes on his
cheeks held the light and his eyelashes were the
darkest of blacks against the pale of his skin.

Once, she had thought the same, Alejandra
conceded. Once, before her mother and her

husband and friends had all been consigned to the afterlife she might have imagined resistance to be worth it, to be honourable, even, and right. But no more. Her heart had been lost to the other side of caring months and months ago, before Juan even, before he had betrayed her and her father for the heady lure of gold and power.

A mishmash of promises had left her grappling for even one honest hope for Spain. All she wished for was peace and a rest from the war and blood that surrounded them. The face of Adan surprised by his death came to mind and she turned it away, unable to bear the image. It could have so easily been her. Or Lucien Howard. It could have been them tonight lying stiff on the cold earth with the pine needles across their faces.

'England is a soft country, Capitán, and far from battle. If I were a woman of Britain, I should never leave it.'

'Come with me, then, when I go. You could be safe there.'

She was intrigued by his words. 'A large promise, *señor*. Too large to believe in, I am afraid, and if it is a choice between battle here or homesickness there, then I think I should always choose the former.'

Unexpectedly he reached out and took her hand and she wished that her nails had been cleaner or her skin softer. Stupid foolish wishes here out in the mountains with the scent of Adan's and Manolo's blood between them and a hundred hard miles to go.

'I appreciate that you are helping me to get home.' His words were quiet and for the first time she could hear a hint of foreignness within them.

It had been so long since someone had touched her with gratitude and kindness that she was overcome with a kind of dizzying unbalance. For a second she wanted to wind her fingers into his strength and follow him to England. The absurdity of that thought made her pull away and place a good distance between them.

'I would have done it for anyone.' But she knew it was not true, that small dishonesty. Right from the first second of seeing Lucien Howard on the battlefield above A Coruña, his long pale hair pinked in blood, she had felt a…sameness, a connection. Unexplainable. Unsettling.

The edges of his lips turned up into humour as he pushed a length of hair away from his eyes.

He held his maps in the other hand with a careful deliberateness and scanned the trees behind. A noise had caught his attention, perhaps, or a bird frightened from its perch. They were too high up for any true danger and the nights without cover were cold. Already the snowdrifts could be seen and if it rained again the ice would form. His breath clouded with the condensation and she felt a momentary panic about exposure. If it darkened and they could not find shelter…

'We have at least five hours before the night settles.' She wondered how he did that, reading her mind without warning and taking the words she was about to say.

A guide, he had said, for General Moore. Penning maps and alone before the main body of the English army as it ran before the worst storm in decades across the Cantabrian Mountains. Even looking at him she could see he fitted into this landscape with an astounding ease and mastery; a chameleon, hurt and exhausted, but as dangerous as they came.

He had bent to lift a dried acorn now, peeling off the husks to let them blow in the breeze. ''Tis nor-nor-west. Another day and there will be heavier rain in it. Sleet, too, if the temperatures keep dropping. Do you know the way?'

Alejandra did not answer. If she got her bearings wrong, then they were both dead. There was very little civilisation between here and Pontevedra and already she was shaking.

Not all from cold, either, she thought to herself. Anger was a part of it, too, that she should allow her worry for this man to override sense.

She could easily slip into the forest around them and disappear, leaving him with his wits to follow and the pine needles and oak leaves to bed down in. But she saw the fever in his eyes even as he held her glance, daring her not to comment, and turned to stride out before her. The bloodstain across his shoulders had widened and every so often a drip of crimson lay on the earth and bracken as he walked.

Chapter Six

An hour later Lucien knew he needed to stop, needed to lie down and reassemble his balance and his energy. His neck ached and the wound had reopened; the warmth of blood had held the cold at bay for a time until it could do so for no longer. Now he felt the shivers even across the soles of his feet.

'We can camp here.' Alejandra's voice cut through his thoughts and he looked around. The clearing was undisturbed by civilisation, with a view wide down across the way they had just come. But most surprising of all was the tall tree tucked just before the overhang, the roots of it providing a shelter of sorts.

'Like a house—' she smiled '—with walls and a ceiling. I have used them before.'

'An oak?' The leaves and structure of the tree were not quite familiar.

She nodded. 'Spanish sessile oak. Different from English oak, I think.'

Lucien put down his rucksack and sat against it. If he had been alone, he would have closed his eyes and tried to regroup, but he could see from the expression on her face that she was already worried by the tenuous nature of his health and he did not wish to add to her concerns. The hardness of the bark hurt and he leant forward a little. He needed to get his jacket off and some water on to the heat of the wound, but in the descending dusk and cold there would be little chance of such doctoring.

'You are shivering.'

He simply looked up at her, unable to hide the reaction of his body further. It was finished, this pretence. He couldn't have moved had his life depended on it, not even if a bunch of marauding partisans were to have charged at that moment through the trees.

'Leave me and go home. You'd have a better chance of surviving if—' She did not let him finish.

'I didn't take you for a quitter, Capitán.'

He smiled because that was what he might have said to her had the tables been turned.

'Besides, you have been hurt before just as badly. I saw the scars on your body when we brought you from the battlefields of A Coruña and if you can survive once, you can do so twice, or a thousand times.'

Her words rattled him. Had it been her who had stripped off his ruined uniform after the battle? He'd been nude beneath the covers when he had awoken in the quiet room that first time, a bandage the only thing covering him.

'Who undressed me?'

'Oh, I forget that you English have such a large dollop of prudishness. War has changed things like that here.' She was rummaging through her bag, so Lucien was unable to determine her expression, though he could hear the humour in her voice. 'Take off both your shirt and jacket so I can see to you.'

He made no move whatsoever to do as she asked.

'Salve,' she explained as she found what she'd been searching for. 'Constanza gave this to me before we left. She said if the wound bled again and you had a fever, I was to make certain to use it.'

For just one moment Lucien thought to simply ignore her and lie down, but the throb in his neck was making his temples ache badly and he knew slumber would be hard to come by in such a state.

Hating the way his fingers fumbled, he unbuttoned the heavy jacket and then the shirt, the fabric of the latter sticking to his skin. When he tugged harder the coppery smell of fresh blood filled the air around them and he thought for an instant he might be sick.

The cold was helping, though, the breath of the mountains soothing and smooth. When Alejandra walked behind and laid her fingers against his shoulder to draw the last piece of fabric away, he started.

'It is off,' she said after a moment, 'and the bleeding has slowed.' Drawing a picture with her forefinger on his skin, she gave him words, as well. 'The cuts are deeper in the middle here than at each side and it is only those ones above your spine that have festered and still bleed.'

He'd been taken from the back. Lucien remembered the first pain as Guy had fallen.

Turning on his horse to fight, he'd drawn his sword quickly, but there had been too many and at too close a range. He had no true recollection of what had happened next save for a vague recall of place. The first true memory was on the field above A Coruña, waking to find Alejandra kneeling beside him and his steed's heavy head across his abdomen.

She washed the injury with cool water and blotted the blood with something soft. The salve held the smell of garlic, lavender and camphor and was cooling. Then she gave him a cup with herbs infused in water taken from a glass container within her rucksack. Its lid was of red wax.

'Stay still while I wrap your wound for protection.' Careful hands went beneath his armpits and then met at the middle. Her breath at his nape was warm and soft and he clung to the touch of it as she pulled the bandage tight.

'You are lucky this was not a few inches higher, Capitán. Nobody could survive a wound that severed the vein there and it was a near thing indeed.'

Close up the green in her eyes held other colours, brown, gold and yellow, and her lashes were long and dark. He had never had these sorts of conversations with a woman before, full of challenge and debate. He suddenly wished that they could sit here and simply talk for ever. The medicine, he supposed, the concoction of some drug that scattered his mind into foolishness and maudlin hope.

He stood unsteadily and put his clothes back on, watching as she arched up, her bag at her feet. A much more sizeable sack than the one he held, Lucien noted, angered by his weakness.

With her hat removed the long thick length of dark hair fell across one shoulder and down towards the curve of her waist. He glanced away. He would be gone in a matter of days and she would not be interested in his admiration. But the green eyes had held his with the sort of look that on any other woman might be deemed as flirtatious.

After a few moments she sat down opposite to him. When she gave him a strip of dried meat to chew he took it thankfully.

'The rain has stopped, at least, but even in good weather it will take us two more days to reach the port town of Pontevedra. More if you become sicker.' The impatience in her words told him she had little time for illness.

'Will your father not wonder where you are?'

'Papa has gone down to Betanzos for a week. I shall be home soon after, using the coastal route.'

'A quicker option when I am not with you, holding you back?'

Frowning, she observed him more closely. 'Are you very rich, Capitán Howard?'

Her question surprised him. Alejandra Fernandez y Santo Domingo did not strike him as a woman who would be so much enchanted with the size of one's purse.

'Your query reminds me of the debutantes in the court of London who weigh up the fortune of each suitor before they choose the most wealthy.'

At that she smiled. 'I was only wondering whether offering you up for a bounty would be more beneficial to our cause than the other option of sending you home. The rebel movement has a great deal of need for money.'

'I have an ancient pile in Kent and a town house in London. Expensive in their own right, I suppose, but not ready cash, you understand,

and all entailed. Other than that…' He spread his hands out palm upwards.

'You are penniless?'

He did not mean to, but he laughed and the sound echoed around the clearing. 'Not quite, but certainly heading that way.'

'In truth, you are blessed by such a state, then. My fortune was what led me into marriage in the first place.' Her teeth pulled at the dry piece of meat. 'Papa chose Juan for me as a husband because he was older and a man of means and power.' Her words held a flat tone of indifference.

'And what happened?'

'I married him in the middle of winter and he was dead before the spring.'

'Because he betrayed your father?'

'And because he betrayed me.'

Her glance held his across the darkening space and Lucien saw all that was more usually hidden.

'So El Vengador dealt with him and you made the marks in the limewash to record his death?'

She nodded. 'I struck them off one by one by one. To remember what marriage was like.'

'And never do it again?'

Tipping her chin, she faced him directly. 'You may not believe this, but in my life men have liked me, Capitán. Many men. Even since Juan I have had offers of marriage and protection. And more.'

In the dusk he could so easily believe this, the deep dimples on her cheeks showing as shadow and her dark eyes flashing.

'But they also know I am my father's daughter and so they are wary.'

'A lonely place to be, that? Caught in the middle.'

'More so than you might imagine, Capitán.'

God. Such an admission would normally have sent his masculine urges into overdrive, but the sickness had weakened him and she knew it.

The moon had risen now, a quarter moon that held only a little light in the oncoming darkness. The noises of birdsong had dimmed, too, and it was as if they sat on top of a still and unmoving world, the tones of sepia and green and grey overwhelming. Far, far away north through the clouds and the mist would be the sea and England. Sitting here seemed like a

very long way from home, though he felt better with the rest and the medicines, his strength
returning in a surprising amount.

Lucien Howard was watching her closely
and had been ever since leaving the hacienda,
the roots of his hair in the rising night filled
with the pale of moonlight.

If he had not been so sick, she might have
simply moved forward and wrapped herself
about him just to satisfy her curiosity about
what he might truly feel like. Juan had been the
sort of man who spoke first and thought about
things later, but this army captain, this English
earl, was different. Every single thing he said
was measured by logic and observation and
there was something in the careful cut-edged
words he used that appealed.

'Are you married?' She had not meant to ask
this so baldly and was glad when he smiled.

'No?' The small inflection he used lifted the
word into question.

'Have you ever been?' She caught the quick
shake of his head and breathed out.

'You are wise, then. Marriage takes large
pieces of one away.' Alejandra was glad that he

could not see her hands fisting at this confession. 'With the wrong person it is both a trap and a horror.'

She'd never told anyone this. She wondered why she was speaking of it now out here in the silence of night. She frowned, thinking that she did know, of course. It was the residue of shame and wrath that still sat in her throat as a constant reminder of humiliation. And it was also because of Lucien Howard's courage.

Her fingers found the cross she wore at her neck, the gold warming in her hands.

'A few people seem to manage the state of holy matrimony quite well.' He gave her this very quietly.

'A fortuitous happenstance that in my experience is not often repeated.'

The deep rumble of his laughter was comforting. She wished she could build a fire to see him better but did not dare to risk the flame. Her stomach rumbled after eating the dried meat and she longed for heartier fare, especially now they would be traversing the high passes instead of the faster and easier coastal roads.

She saw him abruptly turn his head, tipping

it to one side and listening as he pushed himself up. Then his knife was thrown, a single flash in the almost dark, the metal catching moonlight as it rifled across the space in the clearing to fall in a heavy thump.

He was back in a moment with a large rabbit skewered by steel, his eyes going to the dark empty space before them. 'I will build a fire to cook it, but not here.'

Gathering dried sticks, he dug a hole in the ground a good ten yards away behind the trunk of the oak and bent to the task of finding flame.

Alejandra was astonished. She had never seen anyone kill prey with such ease. Even she, who was used to these woods and this clime, would not have aimed with such a precision through the dark. And now they would have a decent meal and warmth.

He was making her look like a woman without skill. Leaning forward, she took the rabbit and brought out her own blade, skinning it in a few deft swipes and laying it back down on a wide clean oak leaf that was browned but whole.

'Thank you.' His words as he threaded the carcass on a stick and balanced it across other branches he had fashioned into carriers. The flames danced around the fare, blackening the outer skin before dying down.

'Will you be pleased to return home, Capitán?'

She caught the quick nod as he rolled the meat above the embers. The smell of the cooking made her stomach rumble further and, hoping he would not hear it, she shifted in her hard seat of earth.

'Did your dead husband ever hurt you?'

The question came without any preamble and the shock of it held her numb.

'Physically, I mean,' he continued when she did not answer.

'No.' Her anger was so intense she could barely grind the lie out.

'Truly?'

He turned the rabbit again, fat making the fire flare and smoke rise.

'Truly what?'

'I am trained to know when people do not tell the truth and I don't think that you are.'

In the firelight his eyes were fathomless. She had never seen a man more beautiful than him or more menacing.

Just her luck to be marooned in the mountains with a dangerous and clever spy-soldier. She should tell him it all, spit it out and see the pity mark his face. Even her father had failed to hide his reaction when he had found her there, hurt and bound in the locked back bedroom at Juan's family house, a prisoner to his demands.

'I think you should mind your own business, Capitán.'

After this the silence between them was absolute and it magnified every other sound present in a busy forest at night.

Finally, after a good half hour's quiet, he spoke.

'Perhaps conversation will be easier again if you eat.'

Taking a small offering from the flame, he split it with his knife, laying it out on another leaf to protect it from the dirt.

Despite herself she smiled. Not a man to give up, she surmised, and not a man to be ignored, either. The rabbit was succulent and well-cooked, but his gaze was upon her, waiting.

'Do you ever think, Capitán, that if you had

your life again you would do some things very differently?'

He took his time to answer, but she waited. Patience was a virtue she had long since perfected.

'My father and youngest brother drowned in an accident on our estate. It was late winter, almost spring, you understand, and it was cold and the river was running fast.' He looked at her over the flames and she could see anger etched upon his brow. 'I couldn't save them. I couldn't run fast enough to reach them at the bridge.'

'How old were you?'

'Fifteen, so old enough, but I made a mistake with the distance. There was a bend a little further upstream. I could have reached them there if I had thought of it sooner.'

Precision and logic. Everything he ever said or did was underpinned by his mastery of both. He had failed his family according to his own high standards, something that was the core of her shame, as well.

'If I could go back, I would have killed my husband the first time he ever hit me. I had my knife hidden in my boot.' She hated the way her voice shook as fury made speech difficult, but still she went on. '"Thou shalt not kill" is repeated in the Bible many times. In Matthew and Exodus. In Deuteronomy and Romans. I tried to take heed of the words, but then...' Her heart beat fierce with memory. 'The second death of hell is not the worst thing that can happen after all, Capitán. It's the day-to-day living that does it.'

He nodded and the empathy ingrained in the small gesture almost undid her. 'You are not the first to think it and you most certainly won't be the last. But you were made stronger? Afterwards?'

'Yes.' No need for thought or contemplation. She knew it to the very marrow of her bones.

'Then that itself is a gift.'

It was strange but his explanation suddenly eased her terror and the truth of the realisation almost made her cry. She had failed to be a dutiful wife. She had failed in her strict observance of the Bible. She had failed in bearing the heavy stick and fists of a man who was brutal in teaching marital obedience and subservience, but she had survived. And God had made her stronger.

For the first time in a long while she breathed easier. It was a gift.

'How long have you been here in Spain, Capitán?'

'Since August of 1808. After a few skirmishes on the way north we ran for the mountains, but the snow beat us.'

'It was thick this year in the Cordillera Cantabrica. It is a wonder anyone survived such a journey.'

'Many didn't. They lay there on the side of the steep passes and never moved again. Those behind stripped them of shoes and coats.'

She had heard the stories of the English dead. The tales of the march had long been fodder for conversations about the fires at the hacienda. 'Papa said a gypsy had told him once that the French will triumph three times before they are repelled. This is the first, perhaps?'

He only laughed.

'You do not believe in such prophesy, Capitán?'

'Generals decide the movements of armies, Alejandra, not sages or soothsayers.'

'Do you think they will return? The British,

I mean. Will they come back to help again, in your opinion?'

'Yes.'

She smiled. 'You are always so very certain. It must be comforting that, to believe in yourself so forcibly, to trust in all you say.'

'You don't?'

She swallowed. Once she had, before all this had happened, before a war had cut down her family and left her in the heart of chaos.

Now she was not sure of exactly who or what she was. The fabric in her trousers was dirty and ripped and the jacket she wore had come off the dead body of a headless Hussar in the field above A Coruña. It still held the dark stains of blood within the hemline for she had neither the time nor the inclination to wash it. A life lost, nameless and vanished. It was as if she functioned in a place without past or future.

Shimmying across to sit beside him, she took his hand, opening the palm so that she might see the lines in the flame. If he was wary, he did not show it, not in one singular tiny way.

'There are some here who might read your life by mapping out the junctures and the missing gaps. Juan, my husband, was told he would

meet his Maker in remorse and before his time.'
She smiled. 'At least that came true.

'Pepe, the gypsy, said that I would travel and
become a hidden woman.' She frowned. 'He
said that I should be the purveyor of all secrets
and help those who were oppressed. Juan was
not well pleased by this reading. His life end-
ing and mine opening out into another form. I
do remember how much I wanted it to be true,
though. A separation, the hope of something
else, something better.'

His fingers were warm and hard calloused.
She wished they might curl around her own
and signal more, but they did not.

She couldn't ever remember talking to another as she had to him, the hours of evening
passing in confidences long held close. But it
was getting colder and they needed to sleep. It
would be tough in the morning with the rain
on the mountains and still a thousand feet to
climb.

As if sensing her tiredness he let go of her
hand and stood.

'The dugout might be the best place for
slumber. At least it is out of the wind.'

But small, she thought, and cosy. There

would be no room between them in the close confines of the tree roots. He had already taken his coat off and laid it down on the dirt after shifting clumps of pine needles in. His bag acted as a pillow and a length of wool she recognised from the hacienda completed the bed.

'I...am not...sure.'

'We can freeze alone tonight or survive together.' His breath clouded white in the last light of the burning embers. 'Tomorrow we will hew out a pathway to the west and take our chances in finding a direction to the coast. It is too dangerous to keep climbing.'

He was right. Already the chills of cold made her stiffen and if the earlier rain returned...

Finding her own blanket, she placed it on top of his. Then, removing her boots, she got in, bundling the other two pieces of clothing from her bag on top of the blankets.

Lucien Howard scooped up more oak leaves and these added another buffer to the layers already in place. Alejandra was surprised by how warm she felt when he burrowed in beside her and spooned around her back.

When she breathed in she could smell him,

too, a masculine pungent scent interwoven with the herbs she had used on his back.

Juan had smelt of tobacco and bad wine, but she shook away that memory and concentrated on making this new one. He wasn't asleep, but he was very still. Listening probably to the far-off sounds and the nearer ones. Always careful. She chanced a question.

'Are you ever surprised by anyone or anything, Capitán?'

'I try not to be.' There was humour in his answer.

'You sleep lightly, then?'

'Very.'

Her own lips curled into a smile.

She finally slept. Lucien was tired of lying so still and even the cold did not dissuade him from rising from the warmth of this makeshift bed and stretching his body out in the darkness.

His neck hurt like hell and he crossed to her sack. The salve was in here somewhere, he knew it was. Perhaps if he slathered himself with the cooling camphor he might gain a little rest.

The rosary caught him by surprise as did the

small stone statue of the resurrected Jesus. She carried these with her at all times? He'd often seen her fingering something in her pocket as they walked, her lips moving in a soundless entreaty.

A prayer or a confession. Her husband would be in there somewhere, he imagined, as would her father. Spain, too, would hold a place in her Hail Marys. He looked across at her lying in the bed of pine needles and old blankets. She slept curled around herself, her fist snuggled beneath her neck, smaller again in sleep and much less fierce.

Alejandra, daughter of El Vengador. Brave and different, damaged and surviving. One foot poked out from under the coverings, the darned stockings she had worn to bed sagging around a shapely ankle.

She was thin. Too thin. What would happen to her when he left? She'd have to make her own way home through the coastal route as she had said, but even that was dangerous alone. What was it she had said of the Betancourts? They hated her family more even than they hated the French. He should insist she go back from here and press on by himself, but he knew he would not ask it.

He liked her with him, her voice, her smell, her truths. He'd have been dead on the high hills above A Coruña if any one of the others had found him, an Englishman who was nothing but a nuisance given the departed British forces. But she'd bundled him up and brought him home, the same rosary in her bag cradled against his chest and her fingers warm within his own.

She'd stood as a sentry, too, at the hacienda when danger had threatened, his sickness relegating him to a world of weakness.

Jesus, help me, he prayed into the cold and dark March night, *and help her, too*, he added as the moon came through the banks of clouds and landed upon them, ungainly moths breaking shadows through the light.

Chapter Seven

They saw no one all the next morning as they walked west.

Lucien would have taken her hand if he thought she'd have allowed it, but he did not make the suggestion and she did not ask for any help. Rather they picked their way down, a slow and tedious process, the rain around mid-day making it worse.

If he had been alone, he would have stopped, simply dug into the hillside and waited for better conditions.

But Alejandra kept on going, a gnarled stick in her hand to aid in balance and a grim look across her face. She stood still often now, to listen and watch, the frown between her eyes deep.

'Are you expecting someone?' He asked the

question finally because it was so obvious that she was. Tipping his head out of the northerly wind, he tried to gain the full quotient of sound.

'I hope not. But we are close here to the lands of the Betancourts.'

'And the fracas yesterday will have set them after us yet again?'

'That, too.' This time she smiled and all Lucien could think of was how fragile she looked against the backdrop of craggy mountains and steep pathways. Gone was the girl from the hacienda who had dared and defied him, the gleam of challenge egging him on and dismissing any weaker misgivings he might have felt with his neck and back on fire and a fever raging. This woman could have held each and every dainty beauty in the English court to ransom, with her dimples and her high cheekbones and the velvet green of her eyes. Beautiful she might be, but there was so much more than just that.

Men have loved me, she had said. Many men, she had qualified, and he could well believe in such a truth. Angry at his ruminations, he spoke more harshly than he meant to.

'Surely they know it was your father who shot your husband?'

'Well, Capitán, it was not quite that simple,' she replied and turned away, the flush of skin at her nape telling.

'It was you?'

'Yes.' One word barked against silence, echoing back in a series of sounds. 'But when he came back from the brink of death it was Papa who made certain he should not survive it.'

'Repayment for his acts of brutality as a husband?'

'You understand too much, Capitán. No wonder Moore named you as his spy.'

He ignored that and delved into the other unsaid. 'But someone else knew that it was you who had fired the first shot?'

'In a land at war there are ears and eyes everywhere. On that day it was a cousin of Juan's, a priest, who gave word of my violence. No one was inclined to disbelieve a man of God, you understand, even if what he said was questionable. I was younger and small against the hulk of my husband and he was well lauded for his prowess with both gun and knife.'

'A lucky shot, then?'

She turned at that to look at him straight and her glance was not soft at all. 'He was practised, but I am better. The shot went exactly where I had intended it.'

'Good for you.'

A second's puzzlement was replaced by an emotion that he could only describe as relief. The rosary was out, too, he saw it in her hands, the beads slipping through her fingers in a counted liturgy.

'You have killed people before, too, Capitán?'

'Many times.'

'Did it ever become easier?'

'No.' Such a truth came with surprising honesty and one he had not thought of much before.

'"And he that killeth any man shall surely be put to death." Leviticus, Chapter Twenty-Four, Verse Seventeen.' Her voice shook.

'You know the Bible by heart?'

'Just the parts in it that pertain to me.'

'You truly think that God in his wisdom would punish you for fighting back?'

'He was my husband. We were married in the Lord's house.'

'He was a brute and any God worth his salt would not say otherwise.'

She crossed herself at the blasphemy as he went on.

'Looking too far back can be as dangerous as looking too far forward in life. In my experience it is best to understand this moment, this hour, this day and live it.'

'It's what got you through, then? Such a belief?'

'I'm a soldier. If I made it my mantra not to kill the enemy, I would have been dead long before we left the safety of Mondego Bay, near Lisboa. No, what gets me through is knowing who I am and what I stand for.'

'England?'

He laughed. 'Much more than that, I hope.'

He looked across at the land spread out before him, its valleys and its peaks, its beauty and its danger. 'Democracy and the chance of freedom might be a closer guess. Spain is in your blood as England is in mine, yet who can say what draws us to fight to the death for them? Is it the soil or the air or the colours of home?'

Picking up a clump of leaves, he let them run through his fingers, where they caught the rising wind and spun unstopped across the edge of the pathway into nothingness.

'We are like these pine needles, small in the scheme of things, but together...' His hand now lay against the trunk of the giant tree on the side of the track, its roots binding what little was left of the soil into a steady platform.

'Together there is strength?' Alejandra understood him exactly. This war was not about Juan or her father or her. It was about democracy and choice and other things worth the blood that spilled into death to defend such freedoms. And was not personal liberty the base stone of it all? Papa had never taken the time to understand this, the residual guilt of her mother's murder overriding everything and allowing only the bitterness to survive.

The waste of it made her stumble, but a strong hand reached out.

'Careful. We are high up and the edge is close.'

She wound her fingers through his and kept them there, wishing she might move every part of her body against his to feel the honour within him. Could life be like this, she thought, could one person be simply lost in the goodness of the other for ever, not knowing where one began and the other ended?

This was a kind of music and the sort that took your breath and held it there around your heart with an ache of heaviness and disbelief. Hope lay in the knowledge of a man who had not given up his integrity despite every hardship.

Such foolish longings made her frown. Her clothes were dirty and the knife that she carried in the sleeve of her jacket was sharp. This was who she was. A woman honed by war and loss and lessened by marriage and regret; a woman whose truths had long since been shaved away by the difficulty of living from one day to the next.

He could only be disappointed in her, should he understand the parts that made her whole. Carefully she pulled away.

'We should go on.' Her voice was rough and she did not wait for him as she followed the path down the steep incline above the mist of cloud.

* * *

She barely spoke to him as they laid out their blankets that night under the stars and the warmer winds of the lower country. She hadn't looked at him all afternoon, either, as the mountain pastures had turned to coastal fields and the narrow tracks had widened into proper pathways.

They had met with a sailor who was a cousin of Adan's and he had promised to take Lucien across to England on the morrow. He'd also offered them a room for the night, but Alejandra had refused it, leading them back into the hills behind the beach where the cover of vegetation was thicker.

'Is Luis Alvarez trustworthy?' Lucien had seen the gold she had pulled from her pocket for the payment and it was substantial, but he had also seen the pain on the old man's face when Alejandra had told him of Adan's death.

'Papa says that those who make money from a war hold no scruples, but I doubt he will push you overboard in the middle of the Channel. You are too big, for one, but as Adan's kin he also owes the dead some sort of retribution.'

'That is comforting.'

She laughed and he thought he should like to hear her do it more, her throaty humour catching. Tomorrow he would be gone, away from Spain, away from these nights of talk and quiet closeness.

'Being happy suits you, Alejandra Fernandez y Santo Domingo.' Lucien would have liked to add that her name suited her, too, with its soft syllables and music. Her left wrist with the sleeve of the jacket pulled back was dainty, a silver band he had not noticed before encircling the thinness.

'There has been little cause for joy here, Capitán. You said you survived as a soldier by living in the moment and not thinking about tomorrow or yesterday?' She waited as he nodded, the question hanging there.

'There is a certain lure to that. For a woman, you understand.'

'Lure?' Were the connotations of the word in Spanish different from what they were in English?

'Addiction. Compulsion even. The art of throwing caution to the wind and taking what you desire because the consequences are distant.'

Her dark eyes held his without any sense of

embarrassment; a woman who was well aware of her worth and her attraction to the opposite sex.

Lucien felt the stirring in his groin, rushing past the sickness and the lethargy into a fully formed hard ache of want.

Was she saying what he thought she was, here on their last night together? Was she asking him to bed her?

'I will be gone in the morning.' He tried for logic.

'Which is a great part of your attraction. I am practical, Capitán, and a realist. We only know each other in small ways, but…it would be enough for me. It isn't commitment I am after and I certainly do not expect promises.'

'What is it you do want, then?'

She breathed out and her eyes in the moonlight were sultry.

'I want to survive, Capitán. You said you did this best by not thinking about the past or the future. I want the same. Just this moment. Only now.'

His words, his way of getting through, but she had turned the message in on itself and this was the result.

He should have stood and shaken his head,

should have told her that the decisions made in the present did affect the future and in a way that was sometimes impossibly difficult. If he had been a better man, he might have turned and walked into the undergrowth, away from temptation. But it had been almost a year since he had slept with a woman and the need in him was great.

'You are not promised to another in England? I should not wish to harm that.' Her question came quietly and he shook his head. 'Then let me give you this gift of a memory, for my sake as well as your own.'

Her fingers went to the buttons on her shirt and she simply undid them, one by one, parting the cloth. Then she leant forward and took his hand, placing his palm across the generous swell of her breast beneath the chemise. The heat there simply claimed him.

She smelt of flowers and sweetness, and the silk of her undergarment against his hand was soft. Her hair had fallen, too, over her shoulder, unlinked purposefully from the leather tie she more normally fastened it with, the dark of it binding them into the shadows of night.

Her nipple was hard peaked, risen into feeling, and the white column of her throat was limber and exposed, a holy cross in gold hanging on the thin chain. He could just take her, like this, Alejandra Fernandez y Santo Domingo with all her beauty and her demons, offering herself to him without demand of more.

'Hell.' His curse had her smiling as she brought the blanket around them, a cocoon against the winter cold.

Her hands were on his neck and his chest, feeling her way. He hated how his breath shook and how the certainty that was always with him was breached with the feel of closeness.

She filled him up with hope and heat, and even the ache of his wounds were lessened by her touch. For so very long he had been sore and sick and lonely and yet here, for this moment above the sea and in the company of a woman he liked, he felt…complete.

Such recognition astonished him as his thumb nudged across her nipple on its own accord in a rhythm that was ancient. He felt her stiffen, felt her fingers tighten on his arms, the nails sharp points to his skin.

'You are beautiful, Alejandra.' His member pushed against the thick fabric of his trousers.

Lifting up, he steadied her against the trunk of a pine, the blanket behind them a shield against the roughness of bark and a buffer of warmth. There was no time now, no dragging moments, no hesitation or waiting. Undoing the fastening of her trousers, he had them down around her knees before she could take a further breath and then his fingers were inside her, sheathed in warmth and wetness, the muscles there holding him in, asking for more.

'Lucien?' Her voice. Whispered. 'What is happening? What is this that you are doing to me?'

'Love as we make it, sweetheart. Open wider.' When she did as he asked he found the hard bud of her centre and pressed in close.

Her shaking was quiet at first, a small rumble and tightening, and then growing. He held her there in the night air and the moonlight and brought her to the place where the music played, languid and true, a rolling sensation of both muscle and flesh.

She was not quiet as she called his name, or gentle as she held his hand there hard inside, wanting all that he would give her, the last edge of reason gone in the final flush of orgasm.

He smiled, his gift to her new philosophy of living for the now and one that would make it easier come the morning. He wished it could have been different. He wished he could simply follow where his hand had been. But there was danger in such abandonment, the least of which was an unwanted pregnancy.

As she slid down the trunk of the tree to sit at the base of it, her knees wide open, he thought she had never looked more beautiful or more content. The smell of her sex was there, too, and he breathed in and savoured it.

'That has never happened before. To me.' Her words, quiet and tearful. Her eyes were full of unshed moisture as he moved his forefinger and the clench of her muscles echoed in answer.

'This?'

'Yes. It was exactly right.'

She was asleep before he had the blanket about them, her head cushioned against his chest. Uncoupling his hand, he sat there and tried to work out what the hell had just changed inside.

Usually sex to him was a quick thing associated with relief and little else and he left afterwards with a small but definite guilt.

But here tonight, when he had not even found his own completion, the tight want in his being was unquenched.

He prayed that this might never stop, this now, here in Spain with Alejandra in his arms. Above them in the gap of cloud a shooting star spun across the sky and he wished upon it with a fervour that shook him.

'Lord, help us.'

It was as much as he could do in this arena of war with a boat waiting to take him home on the morrow and a back full of wounds that were worsening.

Left in his company, she would be compromised and tomorrow when she woke he knew there would be difficulties. In the harsh light of dawn reality would send each of them their different ways and back into lives promised elsewhere. It was how life worked.

Lucien thought of his friends at home and his family and the ancient crumbling estate of Ross that would need a careful guidance if it were not to fail completely.

He could not stay in Spain. He could not

live here. But his arms tightened about Alejandra and he breathed her in.

She came awake so abruptly she jolted and felt him there beside her, lying in the warmth of their blanket fast asleep.

In the early spread of dawn his hair looked lighter again. It was as if more of the darkness had been rubbed away, leaving large swathes of the pale that were caught now in the new morning.

She swallowed back the heaviness in her throat and stayed perfectly still. In sleep Lucien Howard looked vulnerable, younger, the lines of his face relaxed into smoothness. The heavier shadow of a day-old beard sat around his jaw, a play of red upon fair bristles.

She had never lain with a man like him. Juan had been dark and hairy and thick. This English captain was all honed muscle and lithe beauty, reminding her of the statues she had seen once years ago when her mother and father had taken her to Madrid, the marble burnished smooth by time and touch.

She had been astonished at the way he had made her feel last night—still felt, she amended, as the memory lifted her stomach to a tight ache and she moved against him. She wanted again to feel like that, tossed into passion and ecstasy and living in the blinding moment of joy.

He stirred and turned towards her, his hands coming around her in protection, and her fingers found the buttons of his trousers and slipped inside. His flesh was warm and smooth and for a moment she wondered if what she did was right, this plundering, without his consent. Still, as her hands fastened about him the flesh grew, filling the space with promise.

No small measly man, either. No quiet polite erection. Already her hips were moving and her legs opened at the same time as his eyes.

Pale and watchful, the very opposite of his vibrant quickened appendage. The surprise came next, creeping in with a heavy frown.

'You are sure?'

In answer she simply drew him over her and tilted her hips and the largeness of Lucien filled her completely, stretched to the edge of flesh, pinning her there as he waited.

'Love me, Alejandra,' he said and drove in further.

'I do,' she replied, and it was only much later when he was gone from her that she understood exactly what such a truth meant.

He was not gentle or tentative or hesitant. He was pure raw man with the red roar of sex in his blood and a given compliance to take her. She had never felt more of a woman, more beautiful, more cherished, more connected, more completely full.

The way he made love was unlike anything. He used his hands and his mouth and his body wholeheartedly and joyously, as if in the very act he sacrificed his reserve in real life, nothing held back, nothing hidden.

And this time he came with her to the golden place far above, the place where their hearts were melded into one, cleaved by breath and flesh, joined in the sole pursuit of rapture and escape and fantasy. Delivered into euphoria. Like a dream.

The shaking started as quietly as it had done before, at first in the very pit of her stomach and then radiating out, clenching and tight, her breath simply stopping as it spread so that her back arched and she took what he offered with the spirit that it was given, with honesty and pleasure and something else that was more un-nameable.

And then the tautness dissolved into lethargy and the tears came running down her cheeks in the comprehension of all that had just occurred and never might again.

She could not ask him to stay, there was no place safe here for him, and she knew she would not fit into the polite and structured world of an English earl.

This small now was all the time they would have together, close and real, yet transitory. She found his hand. She liked the way he linked their fingers.

'I will come back for you. Wait for me.' His words whispered into the light, the promise within both gratifying and impossible.

'I will.'

She did not think that either of them truly believed it.

Chapter Eight

She was there and not there in the ether of pain and sickness, close beside him in memory and in loss.

'Alejandra?' Her name. Strangely sounded. There was something wrong with his voice and he was burning up.

'It is me, Luce. It's Daniel.' The feel of a cloth pressed so cold it made him shake, first across his brow and then under his arms when they were lifted. Gentle. Patient. Kind. 'You are back in England now. You are safe. The doctor says that if you rest…' The words stopped and Lucien opened his eyes to see the familiar pale green orbs of his oldest friend, Daniel Wylde, slashed in worry.

'I…am…dying?' His question held no emotion within it. He did not care any more. It was

too painful and he was too weak, the wounds
on his neck making breath come shallow.

'No. Have some of this. It will help.'

A bitter drink was placed between his lips
and his head raised. One sip and then two.
Lucien could not remember how he knew this
taste, but he did, from somewhere else, some
dangerous place, some other time.

'You need to fight, Lucien. If you give up…'
The rest was left unsaid but already the dark
was coming, threading inside the day, like
crows in a swarm before the sun. Wretched
and unexpected.

'You have been in England for six weeks. I
brought you up to Montcliffe three days ago.
For the air and the springtime. The doctor said
that it might help. He stopped the laudanum
five days ago.'

'My mother…?'

'Is in Bath visiting her sister. Christine made
her take a break from nursing you.'

Lucien began to remember bits and pieces
of things now, his family gathered around and
looking down on him as though the next breath
he took would be his last one. He remembered
a doctor, too, the Howard family physician, a

good man and well regarded. He'd been bled more than once. A bandage still lay on his left wrist. He wished he might remove it because it was tight and sore and because for a moment he would like to look at himself as he had been, unbound and well.

Alejandra.

The name came through the fog with a stinging dreadful clarity.

The hacienda and the Spanish countryside tumbled back as did the journey across the Galician Mountains. He shut his eyes against more because he did not wish to relive all that came next.

'I thought you'd been killed, Luce, when you did not arrive on the battlements by the sea to get on to the transports home. Someone said they had seen you fall on the high fields, before Hope's regiment. I could not get back to look for you because of my leg—'

Daniel broke off and swallowed before continuing.

'We'd always sworn we'd die together. When you didn't come I thought…'

Lucien could only nod because it was too hard to lift his arm and take Daniel's hand to reassure him and because the truth of battle was nothing as they had expected it to be. So very quick the final end, so brutal and incapacitating. No room in it for premade plans and strategy.

He came awake again later, three candles on the bedside table and a myriad of other bottles beside them.

Daniel was still there, his collar loosened and eyes tired.

'The doctor has been by again. He will come back in the morning to change your bandages as he has taken a room in the village with his brother. He said that I was to keep you awake and talking for as long as I could tonight and he wants you up more. Better for the drainage, he said. I have the same instructions.'

'You do?'

'I took a bullet through the thigh as we left A Coruña. It seems it is too close to the artery to be safely excised, so I have to strengthen the muscle there instead if I am to have any chance of ever walking again without a limp.'

'Hell.'

'My thoughts exactly. But we are both at

least half alive and that is better than many of the others left in the frozen wastes of the Cantabrians.'

'Moore is there, too. A cannonball in Penasqueda. He died well.'

'You heard of that. I wondered. Who saved you, Luce? Who dressed your wounds?'

'The partisans under El Vengador.' His resolve slipped on the words.

'Then who is Alejandra? You have called for her many times.'

The slice of pain hit him full on, her name said aloud here in the English night, unexpected.

'She is mine.'

They had come down in the morning across the white swathe of a winter sun, warmer than it had been and clearer. Alejandra walked in front, a lilt in her step.

'You thought what...?' she said, turning to him, the smile in her eyes lightened by humour. Girlish. Coquettish even.

'I thought you would be regretful in the morning.'

'Of making love?'

'With a stranger. With me. So soon…'

The more he said the worse it sounded. He was a man who had always been careful with his words and yet here they fell from his mouth unpractised and gauche. Alejandra made him incautious. It was a great surprise that.

She waited until he had reached her and simply placed her arms about his neck.

'Kiss me again and tell me we are strangers, Capitán.'

And he did, his lips on hers even before he had time to question the wisdom of such a capitulation here in the middle of the morning. She tasted like hope and home. And of something else entirely.

Tristesse.

The French word for sadness came from nowhere, bathed in its own truth, but it was too soon to pay good mind to it and too late to want it different.

'Only now, Lucien,' she whispered. 'I know it is all that each of us can promise, but it is enough.'

He looked around, his meaning plain, and she took his hand and led him off the track and into a dense planting of aloes.

'It will have to be quick. I am not sure how safe…'

He didn't let her finish, his fingers at her belt and the trousers down. His own fall was loosened in the next seconds and he lifted her on to his erection, easily, filling her warmth and plunging deeper into the living soul of delight.

Nothing compared to this. Nothing had prepared him for it, either, the response of her flesh around him, keeping him within her, quivering and clenching.

He had always held a healthy appetite for the women he had coupled with, not too numerous, but not a puny number, either. Always before he stayed in charge and detached, as though at any moment he had the capacity to pull away and leave. Only momentary. Only casual. He never lingered to hear the inevitable tears or pleadings, preferring instead to depart on his terms, before closeness settled.

Until here and now in the shifting allegiances of war when it was both impossible to stay and dangerous to leave.

His hand cupped Alejandra's chin and he slanted his mouth across the fine lines of her. He wanted to mark her as his, in a primal demarcation of possession. Just as he wished to plant his seed in a place where the quickness might take and grow and be.

The very thought made him come, hot into her, the pulse of desire, the sating of want. He pumped the heart of himself into her womb and held her still so that there might be a chance that part of him would live in her and she might remember. Him.

Dangerous. Stupid. Impossible.

But the rational side of him was gone and in its place stood such a shaking want he could follow no other master.

She had closed her eyes now, as her own orgasm strengthened, panting and tensing as it took her, the flat planes of her stomach as jerky as her breath. He liked listening to her edge of surprise, the red whorls on her throat only emphasising all she had allowed him as the waves of release billowed.

She tried to say something afterwards, but he stopped her because he knew what the words might be and he was not ready to hear them, feel them, know them. Not here in the centre of chaos and pain and delight.

She needed to be away safe and his presence could only harm her if they were found together. Already those on the waterfront might have talked; a stranger with the daughter of El Vengador coming down from the high hills and unaccompanied. Small ports like this did not allow the shelter of anonymity or the chance to disappear unnoticed into a crowd and stay hidden.

As though she could sense him thinking she pulled away, quick fingers retying her buttoned fall. She did not look at him, either, a faint redness tingeing both her cheeks. He could smell the scent of loving between them, pungent and raw.

'We should go, Capitán. The tide will not wait…'

'And you? How will you get home from here?' He could not help but ask, though he held no mandate to shape her future.

'The way I always do. Easily.'

He wanted to believe that. He did. He wanted to think that after he had boarded the boat to England she would simply walk down the path towards home, unmolested, unchallenged.

And if not…

He shook that thought away and took her

arm. 'If you are ever in trouble, send a letter and this to the Howard town house in Grosvenor Square. Do you understand? Address it to the Earl of Ross and mark it as important.' His warm signet ring sat in the centre of her hand, pulled from his finger as the only possession he could bestow on her that was truly recognisable.

She nodded, her eyes had faded into a flat dull green, though her fist curled around the crest engraved in gold.

Alejandra knew as a certainty that an important English earl would have no place beside the daughter of one of the most infamous guerrilla leaders in the northern parts of Spain. A woman who had been married once badly and who had killed and fought and maimed. For freedom, she told herself, but each time took more of her soul and now there was so little left of it Alejandra was afraid. He had not asked about the marks on her wrist, either, the scars of hopelessness and betrayal. The way out.

She would not contact him, she knew that as certainly as she did her own name, but she would keep the ring. These were the last moments that they would be together and she was glad for the wet of him there inside her body, to hold on to and to remember.

The blood was seeping through his clothes again, a dark stain against the navy of his borrowed jacket. She knew how much it would be hurting him.

'Only now,' she whispered at his back. Only this time, she chanted inside herself as the path wound its way down towards the port and to the bright emerald of the sea. He needed medical help and he needed it fast for the heat in him last night had not been all from ardour. A few days to the coast of England in fair weather. 'God, please let it be enough. Please deliver him from his troubles.'

Luis Alvarez was ready to leave, his cargo secured and his sails unfurled. Another man she had not met reefed the ropes at the back of the boat and moved a pile of canvas.

'Is there luggage?'

'No.' Lucien Howard had finally found his voice again. 'My sister married an Englishman and is sick. I need to be there quickly.' She was glad he spoke the Spanish with such precision, for Alvarez seemed to accept his story without pause.

'Come aboard, then.'

She turned towards him and folded her hands across her chest. She was glad this was such a public space, glad that he would not touch her, glad that it was only a matter of minutes before he was gone. Because she could not have borne a dragged-out goodbye. Not after the night and morning that had just been.

'Safe journey, then, Lucien.'

'And to you, too, Alejandra.'

She stepped back and so did he, one foot and then another until the gap between them was such that even had she wanted to she could not reach out and touch him.

Then he was on the boat, gold and black hair blowing in the breeze as he removed his hat.

The noise of ropes stretching and shouts, the slap of water when the vessel turned into the current, shadows and light as the sails slid into shape, filling with wind and then movement.

One yard and then ten.

She did not raise her arms or shout goodbye, but stood there, silent, caught between hope and despair.

'Only now,' she whispered to herself as the shape of him grew blurred by distance and was gone.

His sister, Christine, was there the next time he awoke, her hand across his on the spotless counterpane of his sickbed. She had been crying, he could see it in the swollen redness around her eyes.

'I might live, yet.' It was all he could think of to reassure her and she looked up, a frown across her brow.

'You think that is why I sit here and weep, because you are bound for heaven any moment?' There was sadness in her voice. 'You will recover, Lucien, though the doctor said it might take a while.'

'Then why are you crying?'

'Joseph died before his regiment reached Betanzos. The cold, I think, and a lack of clothing. I got the letter the day after you arrived home and I have heard the stories.' She lifted her hand and showed him a heavy diamond in white gold. 'He had asked me to marry him when he returned and I was waiting...'

'God, Joe Burnley is dead? I am sorry for it.'

His sister detested profanities and she pursed her lips in that particular way she had done so all of her life when one of her brothers annoyed her.

'What? You never swear in your bed at night when no one is listening, Christine? Never rant against the unfairness of it all?'

As she shook her head he laughed and was surprised at how hoarse such humour sounded. 'Then I think you should start. That truth at least is universal.'

'You are so much more cynical than you were, Luce.'

'A failed military campaign does that to one, I should imagine. All the mistakes and the damned waste of it…' He drew in breath. Once he started on the debris of war he might never stop and his sister should not need to learn that her betrothed had died because of an error. Let her imagine bravery and courage and valour instead. Let her think the British expeditionary force under Moore had had a firm plan and a fine higher purpose.

Closing his eyes, he was glad when he heard her stand and leave the room. Grief was a lonely companion after all, hers and his, unexplainable and constant. He imagined Alejandra here looking down upon him, willing him better, challenging him to fight. But his strength had left him ever since he had stepped on to that boat in the harbour of Pontevedra and all he could feel now was an ache of aloneness.

Dislocated and adrift.

The skin on his wrist where the doctor had bled him pulled against the stitching of a blanket and began to bleed again through the bandage as he raised it. One drip and then two against the snowy white of the sheets. He was suddenly reminded of the scars on Alejandra's right wrist, precise white lines that looked deliberate and lethal.

Where was she now? Was she safe? Was she home with her father or out on the hills above A Coruña again scouting? He'd get someone from the intelligence sector to find out the situation there. He'd ask Daniel to organise it come the morning. Then he would return and look for her. That thought allowed him to close his eyes and sleep.

Four weeks later Lucien was back in London and up walking short distances. Oh, granted, he did not have his full energy back or the same sense of well-being he was more used to but he was out of bed and dressed and for that he was grateful.

When Daniel turned up at the Howard town house early after breakfast, though, Lucien knew something was not right. Excusing himself from the table, he bade his friend follow him to the library, away from the ears of others in his family because already he had a fair knowledge of what this visit might be about. 'You have had word from Spain?'

Daniel handed him a sealed missive, but his face looked drawn.

'Is it bad news?' The flat question was asked in the face of disbelief.

As his friend failed to answer Lucien ripped apart the missive, unfurling the page so that the tall spidery writing could be better viewed.

I am sorry to inform you that the Hacienda of Señor Enrique Fernandez y Castro was razed to the ground on the second week of March 1809 and all the occupants within it appear to have died.

These occupants are listed as:...

Both the names of Alejandra and her father were amongst those missing.

Lucien looked up. 'You knew?'

'They told me to make sure you were sitting when I gave you this.'

'Gone.' He read the names again and then again, as if on another try the words might have changed, releasing Alejandra from the spectre of fire.

Crossing the room, Daniel extracted two glasses from the mahogany cabinet, pouring a generous brandy in each. Handing one over, he sat on the leather chair opposite.

'Tell me about her, Luce. Sometimes talking helps.'

Could anything truly help? Lucien wondered as the grief of his loss broke through. 'She was brave and beautiful and fought for my health harder than even I did at the time. She found me the morning after the retreat, under the dead carcass of my horse, and brought me home.'

'Courageous indeed, then.' Lucien liked the way Daniel said that, his tone full of thought and truth.

'She brought me down to the port of Pontevedra and got me on a boat. Then she returned to the hacienda.' He took a long sip of the brandy. 'To die in a fire. I should have insisted that she came with me, to England, where she might have been safe, but she had made it clear Spain was her home and I was…' He stopped.

What? he wondered. What exactly had he been to Alejandra?

'Did you love her?' Brandy words. Careless and exposed and demanding answer.

'No.' Lucien felt his insides curl into grief because he could not say it, could not let the truth become his reality. His fist brought the paper into a tight ball and he was shaking. Fiercely. He wondered for a moment whether this was what it felt like to die of shock. He'd seen others take the same path and it had always been quick.

But then Daniel was there, taking the glass from his hand and lifting him in arms warm and solid on to the sofa to one end of the library, a blanket shoved across the cold.

'Should I get a doctor, Luce?'

'Don't.' He had found his voice again and his wits. Uncurling his fist, he let the paper drop on to the floor, where it sat quiet and tiny, the penmanship unseen. 'Can you burn it?' He didn't want to read it again and find her name there on the third row down.

Her middle name had been Florencia. He had not known that. There were a thousand things he had not known of her and now never would.

When Daniel did as he asked Lucien watched as the paper caught alight in the grate, a small flare of yellow and orange and then gone.

'Was it Alejandra who had your hair dyed black?'

'Yes. She thought it was safer that way. Less obvious. Another protection.'

'I should have liked to have met her. Your woman.'

'Mine.' Now he could not stop the tears that fell unheeded down his cheeks and into loneliness so deep and painful he thought he might never survive it.

Chapter Nine

London—1813

The widow Margarita van Hessenberg was beautiful, clever and wealthy and she was a good friend of Daniel's wife, Amethyst, a woman Lucien both liked and admired.

Lucien had seen her from a distance many times, but of late she had sought him out, to ask an opinion of a book or a play or a painting. A cultured woman with an enquiring mind and a curious nature.

Today in his arms in the Harveys' ballroom Margarita was speaking of the Turner painting that had surfaced at the Royal Academy's summer exhibition at Somerset House last year.

'It was widely praised as magnificent and sublime by any critics who mattered. But for myself the axis of perspective seemed to break with the traditional rules of composition and I could not quite enjoy it.'

Lucien knew that Margarita was an artist and was said to be most practised, but still the painting of the ancient Punic Wars had released something unexpected in him when he had gone to see it.

The image of Hannibal and his army crossing the Maritime Alps with the Salassian tribesmen thwarting them had had a familiar sense to it. The forces of nature he determined, and the smallness of man, caught in war and snowstorms. For a moment he had been transported to his own hell, marching the icy passes between Villafranca and Lugo, the road one long line of bloody footmarks and corpses.

Turner had rendered exactly the despair of soldiers and the loss of compassion. He had placed in the strokes of a brush the exhaustion there, too, and the pain of struggle.

'You are most quiet, Lucien. Do you hold a differing opinion?'

'I liked its power. I liked its terrible truth.'

Her hands tightened across his back as she

moved closer. 'Will you come home with me tonight and stay?'

This was whispered in his ear in a sultry tone and the hairs on his arms stood up at the invitation. It had been so long since he had last bedded a woman.

He should say yes; already he could see Daniel and Amethyst beside him, the hope in their eyes shining like beacons. Gabriel Hughes was there, too, to one side of the room with Adelaide, his new and most interesting wife, and they, too, looked pleased for him.

They all wanted him to be as happy as they were and as content with life and love and hearth. For a good two years now, after the Higham-Browne fiasco, they had paraded one sterling woman after another in front of him, at dinner parties and balls and also at more private soirées especially manoeuvred to make everything conducive to a successful affair of the heart.

And for all that time he had pleaded excuses and found escapes, unwilling to remember all that he only wanted to forget.

Alejandra Fernandez y Santo Domingo.

Even here she haunted him, amongst the

laughter and the dancing, sadness the only honest emotion in his breast. Four years of loneliness. Four years of self-inflicted isolation. Four years of a grief that he could not shake.

And suddenly it was enough.

'Yes, I would like that.' He swallowed and felt the dry fear of the answer in his mouth curling into panic.

'Thank you.' Margarita was clever in her reply. If she had said anything else, he might have bolted, but the sweet gratitude in her words touched him.

'I am not a woman prone to asking men to my bed, you understand.' He smiled as her breath warmed the skin on his neck. 'Once, I was married to a man I loved with all my heart and when he died I could not understand who I was any more. But with you...' The words slid into a silence as he nodded and the music soared in the air above them, promise and hope within its melody.

The substantial van Hessenberg town house was darkened with only a few candles still alight as she led him through the reception area and up the stairs to a room that was painted as a garden, murals on each wall by the windows.

'This is my folly, Lucien,' she said softly. 'I missed my flower beds in Essex and sought to bring them here.'

'Inanimate and permanent? No watering needed.'

She laughed at that and moved closer. 'That is what I love most about you, Lucien. You are a man of few words, but all are well chosen.'

Her fingers went to the tie of his cravat, unwinding it slowly and discarding the length of it on the floor. He watched the white cloth fall and thought of the scars she would soon see, across his neck and back, thick and ugly and red.

'Perhaps we could have a drink first?' The quiver in his voice worried him.

'Of course.' She had heard it, too, he thought as she broke away to find glasses and a bottle of champagne.

An 1811 Veuve Clicquot and the very best of that vintage. He finished almost half the glass before he took a breath and Margarita filled it again.

'I went there once, you know, to France, to

sample the wine in the cave itself. It was magnificent.'

Only the best, he thought. Gowns. Rooms. Wine. Travel. His mind wandered to the dishevelled clothes of Alejandra, torn and dirty as they had marched through the mountains. He remembered the home-brewed *orujo*, too, and small dugout spaces between tree roots, where they had fashioned beds in pine needles under the endless Spanish sky.

He felt less here in a room of so much more. He felt less certain and less strong and less sure. He took in breath and turned to the window, watching the lights of London town and Margarita's reflection in the glass as she walked up behind him.

And he knew without doubt that this was wrong, that he was wrong, that the closeness he had known with Alejandra would not be repeated here.

'I need to go. I am sorry.'

She took his words with calmness and dignity. 'Then I hope you will be back…some other time. You would always be welcome.'

He nodded because the pretence of it was expected and because anything to allow him the chance to depart with some dignity was to be snatched at. He picked his neckcloth up from the thick burgundy rug as he strode to the door.

Once outside the house his desperate haste seemed to slow. He was free. Of the cloying room. Of sex. Of expectation. The night air calmed him, the first hint of winter on the breath of breeze. He should have stayed in Pontevedra or he should have insisted Alejandra go with him to England. He should have done anything other than what he had done, simply getting on that boat home and leaving her to die less than a few days later in the fiery inferno of her home. He missed her. He missed everything about Alejandra Florencia Fernandez y Santo Domingo.

'Jesus, help me,' he whispered as he walked. 'Please, please help me.'

White's was still open. He thankfully found a seat in a secluded alcove and, ordering a drink, leant back against the soft leather.

'Lord Ross?'

A man Lucien did not recognise stood there. 'I am Captain Trevellyan Harcourt, the son of Major Richard Harcourt. I think you might know him?'

'Indeed.' Lucien clipped the word, hoping the young fellow might simply leave it at that. He did not feel like chatting after such a personal and intimate failure.

'The thing is, sir, I have only just recently returned from the Iberian Peninsula. I have a commission in the Seventh Light Division under Wellington, you see, and was sent home because I was injured. Not badly, but enough,' he carried on and smiled.

Lucien could not see where any of this was leading, but he listened because there was something in the young man that others might have seen in him. Dislocation, he supposed, and struggle. Gesturing for Harcourt to sit in the chair opposite, he ordered another brandy.

'I was there myself under Moore, five years ago, in the first campaign.'

'A difficult time, sir, and although the push into Spain was ultimately a retreat it was also important. General Moore paved the way for us.'

'A forward-thinking opinion, Captain Harcourt. There were many who would not be so generous.'

'I take it you made the long march north, then, up to the coast, my lord, and the Bay of Biscay.'

There was a tone in Harcourt's voice that had Lucien sitting up straighter. He knew the sound of a man fishing for information, sifting for details. My God, it had been his job for all the years of his commission with the British army and a prickling awareness of something being important began to rise.

'Why do you ask?'

Harcourt sat forward, one hand delving into his jacket. 'I found this on a finger of a homeless drunk I had a contretemps with and I recognised the insignia. The Ross crest. Your coat of arms, sir?'

Time simply stopped for Lucien. Dead still. Like a crack in the fabric of his world, one moment this and the next one that.

It was his ring, the one he had given Alejandra all those years ago with the strict instructions to contact him if she ever needed help.

She hadn't done that.

Yet here it was again, a little less shiny and

a deep scratch across the bottom of the crest. To determine whether it was gold or not, he presumed, to see if the worth of it held value. How the hell had it escaped the fire?

'It is mine.' Lucien felt his heart race. 'You found it on a drunk, you say?'

'I did. He was a man of dubious means and had a propensity for thievery. I am guessing that the ring was stolen, too, by the looks of him. From you?'

'Where exactly did you come across it?'

'In Madrid, sir, in one of the older barrios there. I cannot remember which. I would not have thought you to come through the city under General Moore.'

'I didn't.' He did not want to say more. 'I will pay you for the return of the ring, of course...'

'I am a commissioned officer, sir, and you were one before me. I should not accept any recompense for returning property that was so patently yours in the first place and one that cost me nothing more than a slight shove to acquire.'

'Then I thank you.' Already Harcourt was rising as his name was called from further down the room; friends, Lucien supposed, waiting for him and wondering why he tarried. Lucien stood as well and shook his hand.

'I am indebted to you. If you ever have the need of a favour…' The other man bowed slightly and moved off.

Left alone, he reached down and took the ring in his fingers, clasping it gently and well. How had such a valuable piece been lost from Alejandra's possession before ending up in the biggest city of Spain? Turning the gold into the light above, he saw a mark on the inside band, an inscription that had not been there when he had given it to her.

Only now.

'God.' A wave of heat washed across him and he sat down.

Had Alejandra survived the fire? She would have had neither the time nor the place to have an inscription engraved on the road back from Pontevedra. Had she somehow turned in another direction and gone south?

His fingers closed down over the ring and he hated the way they shook.

'Please, please let her be alive.'

* * *

Luis Alvarez looked more than a decade older when Lucien finally found him, outside a tavern on the very edge of the port road of Pontevedra.

He'd come by boat from Portsmouth the day before into Vigo and taken a horse on the paths north, careful of strangers and mindful of jeopardy. The war between France and Spain still raged in the north, but the direction of the battles has been pulled east towards the Pyrenees.

The old man's face crinkled further as he recognised him. 'I took you over to England once,' he said. 'The friend of El Vengador's daughter?'

Lucien nodded, ordering a round of drinks and paying.

'I heard that Alejandra Fernandez y Santo Domingo had died in a fire at the hacienda.' He tempered the question in his voice and watched the man directly.

'Aye, a tragedy that. Enrique Fernandez y Castro for all his violence was a good man once. Rumour says it was an act of revenge by his daughter's dead husband's family. An eye for an eye...' His voice fell as he looked around. 'But she was not long gone from here when the atrocity happened and I wondered...' He stopped.

'You wondered what?'

'I wondered if she had escaped it and disappeared altogether for the charred bodies of those left were burnt beyond all recognition and form. It was said someone saw El Vengador's daughter in Madrid a good six months after the fire and another swore she resided in Almeida, but by that time the heart had gone from the hatred of the Betancourts and they just let it go.'

Lucien turned the ring on his finger as the man carried on.

'People say things and see things that are not real. Like the dye in your hair. It was black once, if I recall. Now it is the colour of the sun.'

Placing his glass down, Lucien spoke slowly, feeling his old self coming back, the man that he had been here once. The soldier. The spy. The careful gatherer of information, no scrap of it too small or unimportant.

'Do you remember the exact date of the fire, *señor*?' It had never been noted on any of the reports.

'The tenth of March,' the older man replied. 'My birthday. We were out celebrating when we got the news.'

Lucien quickly calculated time and distance. He had left Spain on the fifth of March. That left five days from Pontevedra to A Coruña. It could be done if she had used the coastal road, but it had rained hard that night out in the Bay of Biscay. Had it done the same here, slowing everything?

'Do you remember what the weather was like that evening?' He held his breath as the old man thought.

'It was pouring earlier on, but it had cleared by midnight. We walked home from the tavern without getting wet, but the mud underfoot was deep.'

The rain meant Alejandra would have had to be more careful. It meant that she might have sheltered, too, in one of the overhangs of a cliff or beneath the gnarled roots of trees until it passed. Unless she had simply pushed on undeterred and met her maker in the hot flush of flame.

He wondered how long she had stood on the wharf watching him go. Others might have seen her there and could remember. He phrased his next query carefully.

'Your son helped you on the docks, didn't he? He was there the day we left, tidying the last of the cargo that you had delivered. A large youth with a beard?'

'Indeed. He is there.' He pointed towards the bar and the same barrel-chested young man materialised from within the forms of others.

'Might I talk with him for just a moment?'

'Keep your voice down, then, if it's questions you are asking. Bringing up the past can sometimes cause problems around here. Xavier. A word, if you please.'

The lad came quickly, a full tankard in hand, and sat by his father. Side by side there was more of a resemblance than Lucien had previously thought.

'Do you remember the daughter of El Vengador, the beautiful young woman who came to the wharf that day with this man?'

Dark eyes flicked across him. 'Yes.'

Lucien took over.

'Did she stay here long in the village after I left with your father?'

'*Sí*. She sat against the mooring post and

of you, too, the other day. I saw her in the park riding and she stopped me. I do not think that family will ever forgive you calling off your betrothal at such a late notice.'

'Clara wanted things I could never have given her. One day she will probably thank me for it.'

'I warned you off her right from the start, if you remember. She would have tied you in knots and fastened on to the side of you for ever without conversation or cleverness. Boredom would have killed you when her beauty wore off.'

'Perhaps.'

Lucien had asked Clara Higham-Browne to be his wife for all the wrong reasons. For loneliness and for a place in the world. Even to please his mother, he thought, if he were honest. Nothing of lust or love or plain damn want. The hitch in his heart made him swallow.

Alejandra.

Her hair down and her shirt open and her hands finding the places in him that melted at her touch.

'How long will you be gone? When do I need to start worrying that you might not be back?'

Daniel's query brought a smile to Lucien's face. 'A month at the least and two at the most. I will be in Madrid.'

'Does your mother know why you are going?'

'No. She was the one who was most taken with Clara Higham-Browne and her family. Mama thought the viscount's daughter would settle me down, make me stay here in England, keep me taking part in the politics of London and the affairs of society. She does not want me back in Spain at least, for a fortune teller once told her I would die there and she is convinced it will come true seeing as I very nearly did. I never gave her the story of Alejandra or the aftermath of A Coruña for she is a woman who likes her children to be near and has a need for the order of her world to be in place. Anyone who challenges that is a threat she wants no part of and she worries until she is sick with it.'

'You truly think you can locate this woman after so many years? In all of Spain?'

'In Madrid. Someone might know something and all it takes is one piece of luck.'

'Good or bad, Luce. Margarita van Hessenberg asked if I had spoken with you. She seemed to think you would visit her again soon. Unfinished business, she said, and I gained the distinct impression she was speaking in the currency of lust as well as the gentler one of hope.'

Lucien turned his head to the sky and felt the sun on his face. 'It is entirely my fault that I let her down. I thought we could be more than friends, but…' He stopped and lowered his voice. 'I need to find Alejandra, Daniel, even if it is just to understand what was between us in order to move on.'

'What of the manufacturing businesses you are so heavily involved in now? Who will look after those while you are away?'

'They will run themselves, Daniel, for I pay the managers I employ well.'

'They seem damned lucrative.'

'They are, though my mother still has her doubts about dealing in trade despite the accrued wealth.'

'Beggars cannot be choosers, Luce.'

At that they both laughed.

Lucien leant back on the balcony of the generous room he had been allotted by the Duke of Palma at his country seat on the outskirts of Madrid.

He had arrived four days ago and walked about the town, feeling the warmth, exploring the central barrios and the palace and the marketplaces in the Plaza la Cebada and San Andres Square, and all the time asking questions that might lead him to Alejandra.

An acquired military intelligence had led him to a man in the district of Puerta Bonita in Carabanchel and this meeting had resulted in the name of a woman who was helping the British cause by sending sensitive information through the closed channels of intelligence.

Señora Antonia Herrera y Salazar was a prostitute in a brothel on Segovia Street in the barrio of La Latina. He had had a discreet servant of the Duke make an appointment with her in two days' time under the false name of Señor Mateo, hoping to procure enough privacy to further his questioning.

If Alejandra was here, she would be helping Spain and its cause of independence, he knew she would be. She would be in hiding, too, for those who had killed her father were dangerous and she would not wish for them to find her here.

Perhaps this woman might have seen her or knew of her. He had to be careful with any physical descriptions because the work was sensitive and dangerous and he did not wish for her to be hurt because of such questioning.

He would tread lightly and hope for some further clue to follow. He glanced down at his newly returned signet ring and felt the hollow ache of loss.

Chapter Ten

Señora Antonia Herrera y Salazar briskly tied the ribbons of her new bonnet beneath her chin and bent to reassure the old woman before her, tucked warmly into a large bed.

'I will only be gone for an hour, Maria. My appointment is at two.'

The lined face lightened. 'You have the papers regarding the loans?'

'I do.' Her fingers touched the soft leather of her bag. 'The numbers in the ledgers are heartening, as well. I looked at them all last night and compared them to our takings at this time four years ago.'

'We have come a long way, then. You and I.'

Kissing the offered cheek, Antonia stood. She could hear the carriage slow at their doorstep and did not wish for any tardiness.

'How do I look?'

'Beautiful. But then you always did, my dear. A companion fit for a king. The younger Señor Morales shall agree to all our requests, I am certain of it. He shall be smitten by you.'

Outside, the driver's eyes widened as she let herself into the hired hack. She had dressed today in the most sombre of all her clothes and yet still she felt exposed somehow, back in the ordinary world of the lives of others.

'I wish to go to the Calle de Alcala.'

They needed a loan because there was no way of expanding their premises without more money and without some form of enlargement and modernisation the Santa Maria *burdel* was doomed to failure.

Other establishments had come to the streets around the port in the past few years and they had not all been fair, the quest for riches in the trade of flesh speaking a language that held no moral scruples. Competitors had tried to poach the women who worked for her and frighten her customers. They had spread rumours and threatened her with retribution.

But Antonia had not buckled and she had never let anyone in close.

Not one. Not even Maria.

She had been good at the details and pos-sibilities that came with running a business. Already she had paid back her first loans and saved a good bit besides. Alberto Morales, the manager of the loan company, had been a help-ful and valued friend, but the old man had died suddenly a month ago and she had heard it said his only son was nowhere near as gen-erous with his lending. Smoothing down the heavy fabric of her skirt, she swore beneath her breath. 'Only now,' she whispered to her-self and liked the calm that seemed to emanate from the two simple words.

Her mantra. The way she lived. Her pathway through difficulty and disappointment. No fu-ture and no past. This moment. This second. This heartbeat of hope and ambition.

Pushing away anything else, she paid the driver and alighted, the stairs leading to the front entrance of the stone building steep and solid.

After introducing himself to her, Señor Mateo Morales got straight down to business.

'Your way of life is rather a chancy one, Señora Herrera y Salazar. I should have imagined my father must have told you that many times.'

'He did not, *señor*. He looked most favourably at my substantial line of credit and often said that if all his customers were as honest as I—'

A well-manicured hand waved in the air and cut her off. 'You are a woman without a husband and one of dubious reputation and residency.' He flipped open the pages of a thin book before him. 'Twice you have not paid on time, and once it was a good month until we received any redress. I am not certain whether I wish to continue my father's arrangements at all.'

Antonia felt as if she had been kicked in the stomach, hard and unexpected. Right from the first day of coming to Madrid, from the first hours of uncertainty and dread, she had known she would survive. But this…?

'Our credit is good, sir. More than good.'

'Our?' He leant forward to read through a page, thin glasses balanced on his nose. 'Oh, yes. I see Señora Maria Aguila is one of those who sing your praises. She, of course, has her own detractors.'

Antonia remained silent, wishing now that the younger Morales might simply say yes and then she could leave, but the atmosphere in the room had changed somewhat and it changed again as he came to stand beside her. Too close. She could smell the brandy on his breath and the lavender imbued in the fabric of his clothes.

'There is a way in which you might make me consider your application a little more favourably if you will, madam.'

She knew what he might say before he said it, the thin grey voice expressing his idea of a good deal without waver.

'If I could visit you, say, once a week for… services, I might be persuaded to look at your request differently.'

'Visit?' She needed to make sure she knew exactly what it was he meant.

'Become a patron of your brothel, madam, and a good paying one, too. I shall be discreet and polite. I am unmarried, you see, and most upstanding, but sometimes…well, sometimes I have the need of relief. I would require all this to be most confidential.'

'And we could well accommodate those desires, Señor Morales. I have a number of girls and women who…'

'No. It is you I want.'

Antonia swallowed. 'You do not know me, sir. At all.'

'But I have seen you for years coming here in the company of my father and I have admired you.'

'I do not think…' She stopped as he leant back to shut the book on his desk with a bang, a frown covering his brow.

'Send me a message when you have considered my request, *señora*. Perhaps when you have had longer to think about it you would be more willing.'

Antonia nodded in order to buy herself some time. Maria was old and sick and the twenty or so girls she employed depended on her for their livelihoods.

'There are other places I could go for a loan, *señor*.'

'Other places that will not touch your business proposition without word from me, *señora*.'

Blackmail. That was how the world ran. I

give you this and you give me that. Money-lenders by nature were narcissistic and vain.

Only now.

'Good day to you, sir.'

Without a promise she turned for the door and walked through it, making certain it slammed hard as she left. The man outside sitting at a desk looked up in surprise at her, but she made herself smile. She had learnt the important lesson of putting a bright face over adversity a long time ago.

'How did it go, my dear? Did we get the loan?'

'The son of Alberto Morales is a charlatan and a cheat and he had the temerity to say that he would only lend me the money if I…' Antonia stopped and brought out the carafe of red wine from the cabinet to one side of the room, pouring herself a generous libation.

Maria's laughter was as honest as it was surprising. 'You are a brothel owner, my dear, not a high-born lady. What did you expect?'

'A business meeting,' she returned with feeling. 'A man who may have acted with more professionalism.'

'I built this place up on consensual favours, Antonia. When I started my body was all I had in the world to barter with and it was a good commodity. Do not be too prideful.'

'I am not for sale, Maria.'

'Not yet, perhaps. But the world in which we live is changing and if you want to continue on here in the capacity that you have been, then a sacrifice is often worth the payment. It is work we have all done, after all, and in the safety of this place it need not be as bad as you think it. A quick tumble with a man who is wealthy, harmless and clean. I can think of worse ways to spend an evening.'

Turning to the window, Antonia looked out. There were beggars across the street, a woman and two children who looked as though they had not eaten in a week. Madrid took in such fallen souls on a regular basis, from the poorer urban outskirts and from other towns on the rural plains and hills when the rains failed and the crops did not come in.

This was the truth of poverty, the line between life and death blurred and thin. Once under another name she might have had choices and options, but here in the old city of Madrid they had narrowed. Oh, granted, she could sell off some furniture and other personal belongings, but the rental on the building was high and nothing would cover the refurbishment costs other than a loan.

She was a brothel owner and soon, very soon, she would be a whore, as well. She knew it would have to come to this eventually, knew that the old ways and beliefs would one day become impossible.

'Very well.' Antonia heard the words come from her mouth as if at a distance. 'Arrange the meeting for the day after tomorrow with Señor Mateo Morales and I will make certain we get a renewal of the contract.'

As she turned, her eyes caught her reflection in the mirror above the mantel, a woman who looked stern and cold, the dyed red of her hair harsh against her face. She could not see what would possibly attract any man to her.

'I want for you to be happy, Antonia, but that cannot happen if we are forced on to the streets.'

'There are more important things in life than being happy, Maria.'

'Important things like the secrets you take from the French, you mean.'

'You know of this?'

'I know of the way you go through the bags and jackets of the French soldiers who come here. I see you watching them, too, and there are rumours…'

'Rumours?'

'It is being said that a beautiful aristocrat is aiding the cause of Spanish freedom on the city streets of Madrid. With Joseph Bonaparte installed in place of the Bourbons and the large portion of Spanish lands under the jurisdiction of the French there is great danger, Antonia. And well you know of it.'

Antonia was struck dumb. She had always been so careful in her clandestine activities. She had worn a blonde wig and talked in the old High Castilian, her face hidden beneath a large hat and dressed in the clothes she had left the north of Spain wearing all those years before.

Capitán Lucien Howard.

He came to her more often now in dreams, which was an odd thing given she had cried for him for at least eighteen months after the fire. It was the days then that were hardest to get through. Now it was the nights.

'Who else knows…here?' The admission was whispered and she was pleased to see Maria shake her head.

'No one. I am old and I sleep badly. I see things that others would not and I worry for you. So alone. So bitter. Is there anyone at all whom you might turn to for help?'

Once, there had been. In the first months of losing her father, her lands and her heritage she had sent three letters to the Earl of Ross. She had kept the ring, though, safe and sound in the pocket of her only jacket, because she could not truly trust another with it.

And she had waited in the hills above the small port of Pontevedra for him to arrive. Month after month until it was too dangerous to tarry further and she had sickened from living in the damp.

He had not come then and he had not come later in Madrid when the fourth letter had gone, paid for in the pawning of her favoured knife so that the postage was secure and the missive had the best of all chances of being delivered.

She had written of her pregnancy and of her

need for help. She had put her heart into the words of entreaty even though she knew her English was poor.

The returned mail had been short and to the point, the crest of the Ross title embossed on to the thick paper.

Do not write again. I shall receive no further mail from you. If you persist in these false claims, I will have my legal team draw up a case against you.

The signature had been Lucien Howard's and the wax seal had been exactly the same as that in the gold of his signet ring.

Then a few months later in the reading room of the library in Madrid she had seen a story of him in an English newspaper. The Earl of Ross was to be married to a woman called Lady Clara Higham-Browne, the daughter of a viscount and reputedly very beautiful. The article had made much of stating that both sets of parents were old family friends and that everyone concerned was most pleased. Alejandra had read it through a number of times, memorising each and every word and understanding that the union would protect the old solid lines of aristocrats who had marched, heedless of any lesser beings, through the centuries.

Her birthing pains had come late in a night in the autumn, a welcomed child, a reminder of all that had been good. But the baby had breathed and then stopped. A boy child and perfect in every way save for size.

After that she had forgotten the promise of the English captain, his troths lost into deceit and distance, and she had thrown her hand in with Maria. A year later the signet ring had been stolen from her chamber at the brothel and she had tossed her rosary into the murky depths of the Manzanares River because she had lost her faith in God and Jesus and hope.

'It could be worse, Antonia.' Maria's voice broke into her thoughts. 'We could be out on the street and homeless. As it is we have fresh beef for dinner and beans from the garden. Life is best lived in the moment, my mother used to say, and I think she was right. Besides, if worst comes to the worst, I can always pawn my pearls and they are worth at least a few months' grace from rent.'

Time was bought in tiny allotments now, here in Madrid on Segovia Street, in La Latina on the land where an Islamic citadel had once stood. The narrow busy streets opened out on to large tree-lined plazas full of tall colourful houses with Arabic-tiled roofs and elegant iron-fretwork balconies.

Home. Safe. Surviving.

Maria was right. There came a time when the line you had once drawn in the sand was shifted and changed.

Señor Mateo Morales, the son of Alberto Morales, was not a bad man or a violent one. He was unmarried and he had needs. If she wanted to keep the brothel, she would have to meet those needs and it had been a long while since she had had enough money to do exactly as she willed.

Morality and integrity were the luxuries of the rich and they were indulgences she could no longer afford to rely upon. Breathing out, she felt her heart break quietly, just a soft slice of pain and then nothing.

Antonia thought she might be sick as she dressed in the light gossamer nightdress that was barely there. Eloisa had fashioned her hair in a series of curls and put on the make-up, thick and garish.

Like a disguise, she mused, like an actress on the stage playing a part. She had so many bracelets around her right wrist and left ankle that whenever she moved she made a sort of music. A harlot's tune. Maria had oiled her skin so that it glowed.

Señor Mateo Morales had asked for an hour. To talk, Eloisa had said, and as the servant dispatched to arrange the appointment he had been grand and stand-offish she had not wished to question him further.

The master did not wish to be kept waiting and he did not wish to be interrupted. The manservant had been most particular about all he did not wish. Privately Antonia thought the younger Morales sounded rather commanding in his stated wants, the thin unpleasant man she had met a week before not quite adding up to one with so many distinct needs.

She looked at the clock in the corner, a few minutes before ten, and swallowed. She was not a young girl and she was not a virgin. She was a twenty-six-year-old widow with scars on her right wrist and a larger one on the top of her left thigh. Imperfect. Jaded. Damaged.

Such thoughts settled her. She could do this. She could. One night a week with a man who was not an ogre or a pervert. One night a week to save all of those who lived in the *burdel* high on the ravine of the San Pedro River before it flowed into the Manzanares.

Footsteps and a knock on the door. A warning. She had insisted on the courtesy because she did not wish to be surprised.

Making her way over to the window, she looked out over the streets and plazas and the outline of the old La Latina hospital a good mile away.

'For all have sinned and fall short of the glory of God…' She had not recited the verses of the Bible in years and she wondered why she did so now. There was no salvation to be had in any of it.

The room was darker than he expected, a single candle burning on the mantel and the rest of the chamber dim. Lucien waited until the servant departed before shutting the door and hesitated again as his eyes grew accustomed to the light.

It was a large and well-appointed room, a place of a well-to-do courtesan, he supposed, the smell of floral oil in the air and some other perfume he did not recognise. Musk, perhaps, or the heavy sweetness of jasmine?

The whore he presumed to be Antonia Herrera y Salazar was standing against the window with her back to him, the gauzy wisp of a petticoat covering little and myriad silver bangles on her right arm. Her hair was bright blood red and fell to her shoulders, the curl of it formal and lacquered. Pearls hung around her neck in one long and drunken strand, the clasp of them hooked into the strap of her chemise to make them skewed.

Rather than speaking he simply stood there waiting for her to turn. Ten seconds and then twenty. She was small, he saw, and thin. All the skin on her arms had prickled into fear.

'I should tell you before we go to bed that I expect you to honour your promises, Señor Morales.' Her voice was high, stretched out into some tone that was forced. The accent was that of León and the north, but edged in the theatrical. 'And I do not allow kissing.'

'Morales?' He could not understand just who it was she alluded to. 'Perhaps there has been a mistake, *señora*. I am here just to talk.'

At the sound of his voice she whipped about, the look of surprise turning to horror before she had gone halfway and then changing again into unbounded anger fired in fear.

'You.' Her mouth was open and her green eyes were wide with shock.

'Alejandra? My God.' He was across the room and taking her arm before he knew it, the velvet of her skin, the grace of bone and flesh. She shook away his touch as if it burnt. 'You are a…a…?'

He could not quite say it.

'Whore.' She supplied the word without compunction, the outline of her breasts so very easily seen against the candlelight. Fuller. More womanly. For a moment through the make-up and the hair dye, through the bangles and the wisp-of-nothing cloth, he completely lost the woman he had once known. 'There are worse ways to survive, Capitán, much worse ways than you could ever know and this is my home now.'

God. He thought he might be sick right there on the bed draped in velvet and covered in pelts of fur. The small cloth on the sideboard told of some cleansing ritual and the oil she wore was so strong it felt as if it clung to him, as well; an essence of ruin.

'Why? You could have been anything or anyone and instead...'

His hands spread across the air in front of her, expressing all that words could not.

'Instead I am this.' Narrowed eyes flickered and flattened, a rise of blood on her cheeks. 'I have survived, Capitán. I have been made stronger by adversity. I am Madam Antonia Herrera y Salazar now, a courtesan and a different woman from the one you knew.'

She lifted a glass to her lips, brandy by the colour, and drank all that was left, trying to dismiss him. But he could not let it go at that. He needed to know what path had brought her here to this choice of a brothel in the back-streets of one of the poorer barrios.

'You had an uncle—'

'Who is dead.' She did not let him finish.

'Then the ring I gave you?'

'Was stolen.' She laughed then, a deep and throaty sound. 'I do not want you here, my lord, paying for a service I once gave you for free whilst preaching on the ways I could have saved myself. I have many customers who like the person I have become, so perhaps it is wiser that you depart. There are others here who could see to your needs and a line of waiting patrons who can most certainly attend to mine.'

Her glance fell to the crotch of his pants and he knew that the erection there was obvious.

'Girls or boys, Capitán? The Santa Maria *burdel* has a large and varied choice. As young as you want them, or as old.' Her voice was hard and brittle and foreign.

Horrified, he could only look at her. The earrings she wore were ludicrously large and made of cheap-cut glass and her breasts spilled over the edge of the thin lace, the nipples darker than he remembered; in mockery and in parody. She was like some tarnished version of what she had been and he could hardly see the girl he had known in the swollen pout of her lips and the unfocused bitterness in her eyes.

He could smell a herb in the air that he recognised and was appalled. 'Drugs? Do you use these now, too?'

'Laudanum. It relaxes the body and fortifies the soul. A useful elixir in my kind of work and I swear there are times when I simply cannot get enough of it.'

Lewdly she spread the silk in her nightdress so that he saw the bare skin of her sex and hope drained from his face when she smiled, the red from the thickened wax she wore on her lips staining her teeth.

He turned for the door and kept on walking.

Chapter Eleven

Alejandra came to in her bed, a wet cloth across her forehead and Lucien Howard gone.

Maria was sitting there, the full light of the midday upon her. 'You took too much of the laudanum last night, Antonia. It has that effect on one who has not tried it before. I warned you one twist of it was ample, but you took three.'

A headache split the day into jagged pieces and she shielded her eyes from the light whilst directing Maria to pull the curtains closed.

'I only took one before my…customer got here and then two more after he had left.'

'Señor Morales does not look like any moneylender I have ever had dealings with. He also does not look like a man who would have the need to pay good money for a woman's company.'

'He isn't Mateo Morales, Maria. Eloisa placed him down as such in the book of appointments and the error was not corrected.'

'Who is he, then?'

'A soldier. An Englishman. My lover. Once.'

'And now…?'

She turned away and let the pillows envelop her. Now she had no idea what he was to her or she to him.

Instead you are this.

His words. The ones that had ripped the heart out of any forgiveness or hope and she had played to his disappointment like a master, pushing him back and keeping him there.

A thousand days of distance had shaped each of them differently and whereas once those differences had fitted them together, now they only tore them apart. In damage and in pain.

One could only be the sum of one's regrets and hers were many.

Clasping at her stomach she breathed in. Their child. She had called him Ross for his father. He had been two minutes old when he took his final breath and the little grace that had still been in her had been extinguished completely. Every day since she had visited the cemetery.

'I will not see Lucien Howard again.' The anger in her tone was threaded in sorrow.

'Then if he comes back, I shall say you have left the house, Antonia. An uncle in Almeida perhaps might be advisable, or a cousin in Cadiz. I have family in both places. I can give him those directions.'

'Thank you.'

Alejandra was gone when Lucien arrived the next evening at the *burdel* on Segovia Street. 'She has gone to Cadiz,' the old lady said, and he had no reason to disbelieve her story. 'She said to say she thought it was for the best, for both of you.'

'I see. She has a place there?'

'Of course. A beautiful woman is always welcome wherever she goes. It is in the nature of men to want to protect such loveliness.'

'Another brothel, then? Like this one? Interchangeable?'

'Antonia was not born with a silver spoon in her mouth, *señor*. Perhaps she enjoys the work. Or perhaps she just needs it.'

'Tell her I will wait in the reading room of the library on the Paseo de Recoletos. I will be there every morning for the next month and if she would like to talk I would like to listen. Give her this. It was hers anyway.' Taking the signet ring from his pocket, Lucien laid it on the small table to one side of the foyer.

The old woman looked shocked as she reached for the gold ring. 'This is yours?'

'It is. I am Major Lucien Howard, the sixth Earl of Ross.'

'Ross?' His title was repeated in a strange manner, almost breathless. 'I will make sure she receives this message, my lord. I promise it on the name of Our Lord and for her sake I hope she will come to you at the library on Recoletos.'

'Can I ask you something, *señora*?'

He waited until she nodded before going on.

'Do the French soldiers come here, to this place?'

'They do, sir. Often.'

'And are you a supporter of Napoleon and his brother Joseph's hopes for the Spanish throne?'

The silence was telling. Spain was a dangerous place these days to confess otherwise to a stranger.

'Thank you.'

He turned towards the door and let himself out, through the garish velvet hangings and a row of poorly painted golden statues. Valour came in different ways, he suddenly thought, and he was sure Alejandra was still here in Madrid for he could feel her close. Looking back at the facade of the house, he hoped he might see movement at the windows, but there was nothing, no telling shadow or twitching curtains.

Was El Vengador's daughter sleeping with the enemy in order to help Spain? He imagined it highly likely as he hailed his carriage. She had been expecting another in his place, that much was sure. Señor Morales was the name she had uttered and he resolved to find out more about the man. Señor Mateo Morales perhaps, for that was the Christian name he had given for the rendezvous. For this moment she might be lost to him, but there had been something in her actions that had spoken of desperation. And sadness.

Tristesse.

As the horses pulled on through the busy

streets of La Latina Lucien swore that he was damn well going to find out what had happened to bring her to this brothel and in a disguise that spoke of hidden danger and hardships.

On the fourth day after the meeting with Lucien Howard, Alejandra went to the pawn-shop on Calle Preciados and got the next three months' rent for the sale of the ring.

It bought her another ninety days and she was not sorry to sell it for it meant nothing any more and she could no longer bear to look at such a false circle of promise.

Lucien Howard had given the ring to Maria as a means of apology, she thought, as an end-ing and a way out. Guilt was there, too, proba-bly, given all that had happened between them. Well, she would take it in the spirit it was given and the pesos realised by the gold would allow her the time to think and plan and be.

Maria herself had been uncertain about such an action because she had fallen heavily under the spell of the English captain.

'You are too stubborn, Antonia. So stubborn you no longer know what might be good for you any more. I do not understand why you will not go to the Paseo de Recoletos and at least speak with him, for he seemed a most reasonable man. I am guessing that he was the father of your child. The sixth Earl of Ross? He gave me his title.'

'My child is gone. Dead and buried. If Lucien Howard had wanted to find me, he could easily have done so. I sent my address and a letter to his home in England, but he did not want contact and he wrote back to say so. It is too late now. For both of us.'

'Because he thinks you a whore?'

'No,' she bit back quickly. 'Because I am one.'

'But you have never…'

'I have drugged French soldiers for my own purposes. I have stolen documents and personal letters and have had no compunction at all in sending these on to those who might pay me well for them. I have taken girls into this house and set them to work in a way that I knew in my heart was wrong.'

'You have always been too hard on yourself, Antonia, since you first came here four years ago.'

'Because once I was not this person. Once I

was better and Capitán Howard only remembers that woman.'

'Does he know you have sent useful intelligence to the British army here? Does he know the girls you employ are well cared for? Does he know the streets in Madrid are a dangerous place for the homeless and the vulnerable and the aged? So dangerous you decided to help by taking them in?'

'He is an earl, Maria, an earl who has a high place in English society. I would only be a hindrance to him, a liability because I am no longer a person he could even like.'

She did not say that her body was different, too, with the birth of Ross. A vain and vapid thing, but still it was there, lurking in the background. No longer young or beautiful. The past four years had seen to that.

'Ross.' Her child. The pain of his name spoken loud had her bending over and sitting. She would not cry. She had run out of tears years ago and Lucien Howard was as good as dead to her.

The vanity of imagining he was here to rescue her, to love her, to take her in his arms and hold her safe was a stupid one. He had been in her room to buy the services of a whore for an hour and no amount of argument could make that different. He was married, too, though she had seen no rings upon his hands when he had visited her.

No. She could not weather another betrayal from a man she had always thought of as honourable and her past would crucify them if she allowed a new closeness.

It was the right thing to do this, for him and for her. She just prayed he would leave the city soon.

The French soldier was fast asleep and would be for some time with the help of the laudanum she had administered. Eloise, one of the younger girls, was in his bed curled around him to keep him quiet whilst she rifled through his clothes behind a curtain hung specially to one side of the room for just this purpose.

It was so easy to catch them off guard, these boys, Alejandra thought, so simple to allow them a few indiscretions whilst toasting king and country and their hopes for an empire that would rule the civilised world.

There was only a small paper in his pocket

as she went through the jacket and it was in code. She had seen these before, the jumbled nonsense of war secrets written so that no one else, save the proper receiver, could understand them.

Sitting at her armoire, she meticulously copied the scrawl, making certain that every letter was exactly the same and that each line reflected precisely what was written there. The English would pay well for this and the soldier for all his youth had a jacket with many decorations upon it.

Tucking the letter in her diary and placing it in the secret drawer at the back of her desk, she returned the original document to the particular pocket it had come from and signalled to Eloise that her search was finished. He would wake soon and then…

The door was torn open and it hung drunkenly on its hinges. There was the sound of crying and screaming from further within the house and a group of French soldiers here in her room.

'Come here.' The first man gave the order and Eloise scrambled to her feet to hide behind Alejandra as two others came forward. In her nightgown the young girl was at a distinct disadvantage, the thin lacy fabric of the thing stretched across her breasts so that everything was exposed.

'It is me you need to speak with, *monsieur*. The girl here is young and an innocent—'

The older officer slapped her across the face, hard, and Alejandra tasted blood and fear at the very same time, though she was pleased when Eloise was allowed to run from the room.

'It is you I particularly wish to speak with, Señora Antonia Herrera y Salazar.'

His glance took in the young soldier naked upon the bed and the clothes he had been in folded neatly across a nearby chair. He found the document within a moment and held it up to her.

'We have word that you are a spy for the English and that you are using this place as a means to steal intelligence from any military man who has the misfortune to use your establishment. You drug them? Is that how it is done?'

'No.' She sought for feminine wiles and abject terror. 'I am only a working woman and he is asleep.'

'Wake him up.' A barked order to a fourth man, who promptly shook the boy on the bed violently. He remained in slumber.

The first man hit her again. She felt the smack of his hand across the bridge of her nose and wondered if perhaps it was broken. At least he had not smashed in her teeth.

Maria was suddenly there, the old woman fighting her way through the crowd with her stick raised.

'Leave her alone. She has done none of the things you say she has. She is a good girl and—' Someone pushed her away and she fell, slowly, one moment there with her anger and her concern and the next falling, her head striking against the sharp brick corner of the fireplace as she went down and then silence.

It was as if Alejandra was in a play, not quite real, the fantasy of horror and blood and glassy eyes. Death held a look that she had seen many times over and here it was again in her room, beside the thick burgundy velvet of the curtains and on the waxed boards of the floor, the polished stick turning in its own macabre circle before it slowed and stopped.

She tried to get to her, to pull away and cradle the woman who had taken her in, pregnant and terrified all those years before, to give her a home and a place of safety. But the older man simply walked forward and without saying a word removed his pistol from his pocket and slammed it down across the back of her head.

She woke in a cell and she was naked. It was dark and she was shivering violently, from fright rather than cold, she thought, though small tufts of straw were the only barrier between her and a rough dirt floor.

Maria was dead. It was finished, this part of her life, and she had heard what happened to women prisoners taken by the French. Many did not return and if they did they were seldom the same. War held a violence that would never have been acceptable in peacetime and a spy couldn't expect a pleasant time of it. They would have found the copied note by now and the laudanum held enough evidence for them to be certain of her guilt.

She had not been raped yet. Her head was sore and there were scratches on her breasts. Her nose ached and her cheek stung, but apart from that... She ran her fingers across herself just to check and found nothing more than a badly split bottom lip.

It was either very late or very early, the darkness complete and thick. The cell held no window and the walls were all of stone. She wondered if she could start digging, but the ground was as hard as any rock and she knew that she would need to conserve her energy for what would come next.

She was not afraid of dying.

That thought came with a surprising certainty. There was nothing left here for her now that Maria was gone and Ross was there on the other side waiting.

She wished she might pray, might find the words that used to mean so much to her, the guidance and the truth, but even as she started to recite the Apostles' Creed she stopped. God would know she did not mean them, could not mean them, because her heart had been shut off to that succour for years, the falsity of it so very obvious.

A noise held her still, a small quiet sound that came from the left down a dark corridor. And then Lucien Howard was there on the other side of the heavy iron gate, dressed in black like a shadow, a slouchy hat pulled down low across his hair.

'Shh.' He did not say a word as he lifted the lock and fitted it to a thick wire he held in his hands. Two seconds and the catch released. Opening the door, he drew her out, whipping a blanket around her shoulders and head so that she was like a wraith in the night. He wore gloves, thin leather ones that felt warm against the skin of her arms where he held her.

She could barely see where they were going it was so black, but he moved like one who could find the way and soon a new corridor appeared.

'This way.' His first real words. She stood on something and it cut her foot. She felt the slice of it and the pain, but did not say a thing.

Then he was lifting her through a window and out into the cool of night, where she fell a good few feet on to the softness of long grass and earth and rolled to the bottom of an incline.

They ran as fast as they could go across the wide openness of the ground around the building, away from the high stone walls and silence, up into the hills and early-morning light, stopping only as the cover of the bushes became thicker.

'Hell.' He was looking at her foot and the trail of blood she had left behind her. 'When did this happen?'

'In one…of the…corridors.' She was so breathless she could hardly give him answer. He simply pulled her up then and wrapped his cloak about her foot and carried her on into the morning until they reached a stream.

'Stay in the middle of the water and don't touch any of the branches.' He did not wish for broken twigs or torn leaves, but she understood that well and was careful in her progress.

One hour and then two and then two more, the sun full up into the sky now and her throat burning with thirst. They had left the river a few hours ago and were now well out into the countryside. The water had stopped the bleeding and all that was there now was a dimpled white jagged line of skin, sealed off by the cold.

He handed her a flask he'd filled from the stream and she drank until he took it off her and drank himself. Then he turned to her, the look in his eyes angry and distant. She tucked the blanket over her shins to cover any piece of skin that was showing.

'Right. Now, Señorita Alejandra Fernandez y Santo Domingo, you are going to tell me exactly what the hell just happened and why you were in a Spanish brothel pretending to be a whore.'

'Pretending?'

'Enough.' This time she heard more than only indifference. This time the man she had known in the north of Spain was back, too, careful, still and clever. 'I came to save you from the French because you did the same for me, once, but it seems you have been selling secrets to the British army for the past three years.'

He brought a paper from his pocket and she saw it was the same coded document she had copied out…yesterday? Or was it the day before?

'It is a wonder the French didn't find this. A secret drawer in a desk is hardly difficult to locate. A woman at the brothel told me you were the owner and that you did not service patrons.'

'Did she also tell you Maria is dead, the old woman who I work with? The French soldier killed her so easily when…' She stopped because she could not go on. 'What now? What happens to me now?'

'I am no longer with the military for I resigned my commission after A Coruña, but I will take you to the British in the north. You will be safe there.'

He promised her nothing more. He had saved her because she had done the same for him and now…now they were people travelling in directions that the other could not follow. Still, she could not quite give up.

'I wrote to you. In England. But you know that.'

His head tipped and he stilled. 'No letter ever found me. When was this?'

'After you left Pontevedra. And then again when I first arrived in Madrid. I wrote to tell you…' She just could not go on. Not like this, not in fright on the run and a scowl on his face. Not when he was looking at her as if she were a stranger, a foreigner, a woman whom he no longer recognised.

Ross deserved more than that, more than a quick mention and an instant dismissal. Someone had written back to her, though, and if it was not him…? His family, perhaps, horrified that a girl of no title who wrote in broken English might claim the Earl of Ross as the father of her illegitimate child.

'I was sick for a long time when I arrived back in England. Perhaps the missive was lost.'

'Perhaps,' she murmured back and took in breath. She'd burnt the letter she had received from London with the seal of an important earldom upon it and the words that had broken her heart.

Suddenly it all seemed like a long time ago and she was so tired she felt as if she would just fall down to sleep for a hundred years, like that princess in a folk tale her mother had told her once.

But she was not a princess. She was a runaway and a traitor. She was also broke, naked and hurt.

'You need to sleep.' He had been able to do this before, to read her mind and find the solution to the problems of it. 'I will find you some clothes at the next town we come to.'

'Thank you, Lucien. For everything.'

Even if it was not love that had brought him to the French prison she could not imagine what might have happened in the morning if he had not come. The hugeness of such a risk made her stomach feel sick. If they had captured him, too…

She wished he might touch her as he used to, just once, but he did not. The scowl on his face was distinct.

They had moved nor-nor-west at night when dusk fell and the moon rose. He had found her clothes and boots in a small village in the afternoon of the first day and she was dressed as a lad because it was less conspicuous and much safer. The next morning they boarded a public coach going north on the Burgos Road.

He seldom really looked at her, his whole being focused on the journey and their safety. The intimacy that they'd had was gone and in its place sat a shared wariness.

She did not mention the letter and the reply and he did not ask her anything of her time in Madrid. A strained truce of acceptance ensued, the fragile new shoots of trust too young and small to be battered again by revelation and survive.

They skirted around other more impersonal issues, though mostly there was silence.

The fire at the hacienda came up on the fourth day of travelling as they moved north from Burgos and towards the coast.

'I thought you were dead. The documents of the fire I saw in London mentioned your name beneath your father's. There were no survivors. No one was left.'

'It was the Betancourts,' she said, lifting her glance to his. They were sitting beneath the overhanging boughs of a large oak just outside San Sebastian and it was almost dusk. 'The family hated us after Juan's death and I think they saw their chance and took it. The fight that killed Manolo and Adan was a part of their revenge, I suppose, as well. Did your report mention what happened after the fire?'

'No.'

'Not everyone perished in the house. When they came out from the hacienda they were shot and their bodies tossed back into the flames.'

'Where were you when this was happening?'

'Returning on the high pass from Pontevedra. It had been raining heavily and I had to wait until the weather cleared to get through.'

'Then who told you of it? Of the aftermath, I mean. Of the fighting?'

'Tomeu escaped and he came to find me. He was burnt badly, trying to save my father, and died four days later for I had very little to tend him with and dared not risk going down into the village again. I spent a night watching the house from the hill behind after he had passed and saw that the land was empty, of men and livestock. Then I left.'

'You went alone?'

'I did. I travelled south to Madrid and cut my hair and bleached it. I found new clothes, a new voice and a new name.'

She did not mention the fact that she had returned to Pontevedra and waited many more weeks for him in the hills above, praying to God all the while that he might come back and save her.

In the last light of the day Lucien saw other truths that she was not saying, darker honesties that left the green of her eyes locked in hurt.

The colour of her hair was a bright and artificial red. He wished she had left it just as it was, long and dark and shining. He wished, too, that she might look at him properly, the furtive short glances beginning to annoy him. Only a few times had she lifted her chin and met his eyes directly, but the challenge and the strength he had always associated with Alejandra Fernandez y Santo Domingo was gone, an indifferent resignation at her lot in its place. A watered-down version of the girl he had once known, wary, plaintive and sad.

Her hands, too, were so much more still. Her rosary was missing and when she spoke her fingers hung now by her side, lifeless and quiet. Each nail was coloured in a redness to match her hair, though the paint was chipped badly with the exertion and hardships of the past days. He wondered how one removed such lacquer so that the vestige of anything left was gone. She had worn gloves in the carriage up to Burgos and a large cloth hat that had hidden most of her face and hair. She walked like a lad and acted as one, too. A chameleon, changed beyond belief.

Her right wrist was still crossed with the scars he had seen there before and although she saw him looking she did not try to hide them as she had always done in the hacienda above A Coruña or in the mountains of Galicia.

This is me, she seemed to wordlessly say. *Battered and ruined. Take it or leave it. I do not care.* The buttons on her shirt were done up to her throat in a tight marching line despite the heat and the collar of the jacket she wore at night was raised around her neck. Concealment. She wore it like another set of clothes.

'Did you bury your father?'

'No. I left him where he was, for all the bodies were charred beyond recognition and I could not risk being seen there. When I travelled the acrid smell of burning followed me for miles.'

He thought she might cross herself or recite some appropriate and known verse of the Bible, but that was another difference. In the five days of her company he had not seen her once murmur a Hail Mary or hold her hands up in silent prayer.

It was as if the changes in her appearance outside were mirrored in the inside traits. She had never asked him even one personal question about his own recent past.

'Do you still carry a knife?' His own query was out before he could stop it.

'No.'

'Never?'

For the first time in his company since leaving Madrid she smiled, a nervous and measured humour, but undeniably there. He was heartened by it and pressed on.

'You have lost the skill of wielding a blade?'

'More the inclination, I think, Capitán.' A quick surge of anger accompanied her reply. He covered the silence quickly.

'I do not know whether to be relieved or concerned by that.'

'At least you have no worry of a dagger through your ribs in the dead of night.'

Only in my dreams, he thought and stood, the conversation getting too close to the bone.

He had wanted her before and he still wanted her in the way a man needs a woman. He shouldn't and he hated that he did, but there was no help for it.

'It is time to go.'

Scuffing at the ground in which they had lain, he picked up his bag. The bruises on her face were fading and the black beneath her left eye was changed to a lighter tone. Her bottom lip still looked puffed and split, but he'd had the same at A Coruña after the battle and he remembered that had taken a long while to heal.

All in all she had been lucky. At least they had not used their knives on her and everything would mend. The sunset tonight was a vibrant yellow, the branches of the trees outlined in the stillness so that every leaf could be seen against the glow. A moment in time and yet out of it, he thought, a moment remembered for its quiet peace and beauty amongst all the danger, chaos and change.

Chapter Twelve

Lucien Howard had always had that knack of full certainty, she thought as she watched him check his compass and look up at the sky. He had been the same in A Coruña, and on the road across the Galician Mountains, and here he did not falter or hesitate as he pushed forward through the scrub-filled hills in the moonlight.

She had no idea as to where they were headed, but he had said he would take her to the British camp and she knew the army under Wellington to be somewhere in the vicinity of the northern coast towards the east.

The smell of smoke was barely noticeable at first, a slight wisp of burning on the air. She knew he had smelt it, too, for he stopped, his face lifting into the wind.

'San Sebastian is on fire.'

Shocked, Alejandra could only nod, for tall billows of smoke crested a hill, the black height of it denoting great damage. They could hear no gunshots or sounds of fighting, though, as they crouched down on the top of the hillock and waited, the early-morning sun on their backs and a thousand questions unanswered. Below there was the movement of people along the streets and the carts of an uninterrupted trade.

'It is over, the battle. I think it's the vanquishers who have started the fire.'

'The English, then? They have won it?'

'If they had not, we would see them still outside the fortified southern walls or across the estuary of the river. It is Rey who is the general in charge of the French here and they have used the ancient fortifications well for defence by all accounts. But Wellington has over nine thousand men from Oswald's Fifth Division and a good number of Portuguese troops to boot and Rey has only just on three thousand. So San Sebastian was always going to fall if Soult didn't have the means to defend it, which he hasn't for word has it they are a lot further east in the foothills of the Pyrenees.'

Such words told Alejandra that Lucien Howard was still involved in the military somehow. She stayed silent whilst he removed a small looking glass from his bag and pieced it together before aiming it towards the city walls.

Finally he stood. 'Come. We will go down and make ourselves known for I am fairly sure it is the English who are in charge.'

The town was reeling with drunken riotous mobs of British soldiers, the brandy and wine flowing freely in the streets.

Lucien made certain that Alejandra stayed close behind him, glad she was dressed in her lad's clothes. Down nearly every alleyway and small lane there was evidence of violence, men with their throats cut and the screams of young women heard. Rape had a certain sound to it unlike the silence of murder.

When a half-clothed girl ran into him as she tried to escape a trio of drunken English louts, Lucien held her arm so that she did not fall.

'Help me.' The words were only mouthed as though sound had been taken from her in shock. Pushing her behind him, he confronted those who stood now watching.

'She's our Spanish whore. Give 'er back and get yer own, guv. There's plenty of 'em here.'

Drawing his pistol, Lucien pointed it straight at the heart of the biggest man.

'You'll have to take her from me first.' All these soldiers understood was aggression and his anger had surfaced in a red-raw fury.

When the same man came forward with a knife, Lucien simply shot him above the knee, in a fleshy part of the leg, a small injury that would not permanently disable him, but would certainly hurt. Then he lifted his gun to another behind, threatening to do the same again.

'Good shooting.' Alejandra's voice was close.

The piercing screams of the girl between them almost drowned out the barrage of swear words directed at him by the departing English soldiers, yet as chaos consumed them Lucien was more and more aware of the calm surrounding Alejandra. She did not flinch or pull back. No, she stayed right behind him, resolution to aid him well on show, even weaponless.

No doubts. No misgivings. She had taken

the Spanish girl by the hand and was trying to give her comfort, settling her with quiet words of strength.

'They are gone now and they won't be back.'

She could not say more for at that moment an older man came from a house a few yards away, tears streaming from his eyes.

'I thought you were dead. I thought that you had been taken away.'

'Papa.' The girl rushed into his arms. 'This man saved me. He shot the drunken soldier and frightened the rest.'

'Then I thank you, sir. My daughter is all I have left and without her...'

More shouting further away had them turning and the pair disappeared into their house, the heavy door closing behind them. Lucien hoped such a protection would be enough, but he doubted it. He had never seen such lawlessness and lack of organised control in all his years in the army. He turned to Alejandra, her green eyes watchful and the fury all about them still.

'We'll need to find Wellington and his aides, for he will know me, but this is a dangerous place, Alejandra, so stay close.' Reaching into his bag, he brought out a knife he knew she would recognise, wicked sharp, the heft smoothed from years of use.

'Take it and don't hold back if you need to use it.'

The look and the feel of the weapon in her fingers was familiar. For so long she had carried a knife. Until Madrid when death had reduced her to not caring whether she lived or died and so such protection was immaterial.

For a moment, though, some small thing came back, some stronger sense of herself, a knowledge of who she had been once. Before. It was the knife she had given him at the hacienda in the very first days of his arrival there.

'If anyone attacks you, kill them. There are no rules here save anarchy and it is a choice between your life or theirs. An eye for an eye and a tooth…'

'I no longer believe in any of that.'

'God. Jesus. Heaven. Hell?'

'Hell, perhaps, but none of the other.' The feeling in her throat thickened as she said it. Once, religion had been her backbone and her strength. Now it was lost to her, through both choice and circumstance. 'Look about you, Capitán, and tell me, is there a God here, in this?'

'Maybe,' he replied. 'Maybe in the lesson of it for next time, I think.'

She glanced away because in his simple philosophy she saw the truth of who she had become and also of who he was.

She wanted to ask him then what his life had been like across the past four years, but she did not. Safer that way, she thought, holding on to her distance like a shield as she positioned the knife in her fist.

The wholeness she had felt with him all those years ago was creeping in again. Unexpected and wonderful. The fears and struggle of life seemed to melt away in his company and all she felt were the possibilities. Swallowing down the hope of it, she followed him into the town proper.

'It's a damned mess, is what it is.' Ian Mac-Millan, an aide of Wellington's, had taken them into the house used by the officers on the far side of San Sebastian. 'Our casualties were high in the first onslaught from the beach because although the town wall was breached there was a second inner *coupure* that meant those sent in were trapped in a no man's land. Many died there and the anger has lingered. This is the result.'

'The wine and brandy has something to do with it, too, I am guessing.' They'd seen casks on the street upturned and abandoned so that the liquid was running in the gutters, the colour of blood.

The other man nodded. 'Indeed, the place was full of booze and the men have run amok, pillaging, burning and killing. Some of the officers tried to stop them, but they were either ignored or threatened. Sanity is long gone.'

'And it will be this way until the alcohol runs out.' Lucien stated this quietly as he looked out the window across a plaza filled with violence. 'Where are the French now?'

'General Rey and his men have retreated to the hill of Urgull, a small garrison on the mound above the beach. The Marquess of Wellington is expecting them to ask for terms as they are surrounded, and as I think he has not the heart, after this, to beat them down further, he will agree.'

'It's been a long campaign, then?'

'As long as yours was, sir, under Moore. We heard about the difficulties in that one.'

'At least you have had your victories.' His humour was measured as the sounds of those outside filtered into the room.

Captain Howard was not dressed as a soldier, but anyone looking at him could tell he had been one. It was inherent in the way he stood and spoke and in the questions he asked. He was not bent down by life or death or even by what had happened here. He had saved a young girl today from being raped and shot a soldier in the knee and yet he had made no mention of this to anyone.

Honourable and good. That was who he was and the anger that had built a tight knot about Alejandra's heart began to loosen.

'Would you and your lad like a bed here tonight? It might be safer than taking your chances out there at least.'

It was getting late and a storm looked to be brewing to the north. Lucien caught her eye in question and she nodded.

Four hours later they were finally alone, the dinner an early one and quickly taken.

Two beds stood against each wall and although the room was small it was cool, a band of windows along one side open to the night and two storeys up.

With the candles burning and a bottle of wine on the table between them this place was the most luxurious and private accommodation they had had since leaving Madrid, but it made Alejandra feel nervous. With her anger slipped a notch she could no longer latch on to fury as a way to keep Lucien Howard at a distance. Yet he had not in one word or touch signalled he wanted more than the relationship that prevailed.

Cordial. Wary. Polite.

Taking off her hat, she fanned her fingers through her hair and spread the heavy heat of it out before tying it up with leather.

'Will you dye it again?'

This was the first truly personal question he had asked her.

'My hair?'

He nodded and sat down on the opposite bed watching her. 'Do you prefer it that way?'

'The blonde I used to have was worse.'

At that he laughed.

'Maria insisted on the red because her daughter had been one. She had bottles of the stuff left after Anna passed and I suppose I was her substitute.'

'How did she die?'

'Giving birth. It is a dangerous thing to do and sometimes a mother can perish, or a…'

Stopping herself by sheer dint of will, she felt the tremble of loss run over her heart. A child could die, too. So very easily. Her child. Their child. Left in a nameless grave in a cemetery she might never be back to visit.

And yet here…here the disasters of life were unfolding about her, too, and Lucien had kept her safe, untouched, whole. The fright of the young girl had shocked her, the relief of her father amidst screams and shouts of other victims in all the corners of the town underlying the terror.

Death visited unannounced and with little warning. One moment here and the next one gone. Like Ross. Like her father. Like Maria and Tomeu and Adan and Manolo and her mother. It took no account of honour or fairness. It just was.

Five days ago she had cheated it in the dank

and cold prison cell on the outskirts of Madrid and tonight she lay above the chaos and looting in San Sebastian, yet cocooned in safety.

Lucien Howard was sitting with his back against the wall, having removed his boots and jacket. His knife was laid down next to him, in the soft leather in which he sheathed it. 'The battle for the freedom of Spain is nearly won.'

'At a great cost to the town of San Sebastian,' she replied, watching him frown.

'"Only the dead have seen the end of war",' he quoted. 'Plato said that more than two thousand years ago and it still holds true today.'

'The philosopher?' She had heard of him but had read none of his treatises. 'You are a learned man, Capitán, yet you are not a soldier any more? You no longer march with your army?'

'No. One needs heart to fight well.'

'And yours is lost? Your heart?'

He met her gaze at that and for a moment through the final slash of light before the darkness fell she saw what war had cost him. It was written on his face in sadness and loss. As it probably was, just as distinctly, on hers.

Turning away, she pulled back the sheet and

kicked off her own boots even as she fashioned a pillow from her jacket. She was glad for the night-time and the privacy it afforded as she lay down.

'What will happen next, do you think? With the English forces?'

'It is most likely that Wellesley will chase General Soult across the Pyrenees and back into France and Joseph Bonaparte will be sent home from Madrid as the support for Napoleon crumbles. Another year should do it and then there will be nothing left of the little Emperor's pretensions.'

'Just dead people,' she said quietly, 'and sadness.'

He wished he could have gone outside and walked, but he did not want to leave Alejandra here alone and so he lay back in his bed by the window and watched the clouds instead, scooting across the moon and running just ahead of a storm.

What the hell was he to do with her now? He could not simply hand her over to the British army's safekeeping with the confusion here and the French less than a mile from where they lay. Her disguise was at best tenuous and he had the suspicion the aide to Wellington who had shown them to their room had already understood the lad who accompanied him was indeed a lassie.

Lifting a glass from the table, he drank some of the wine, a fine and full-bodied red with a strong hint of something he could not quite define.

Like Alejandra, he smiled and looked over to where she lay.

He had watched her sleep in the hills after A Coruña and she still slumbered in the same way, curled up on her side with one hand under her head. The bandage on her foot was dirty where she had kicked off the sheets to allow a freedom and he vowed to find a medic on the morrow to get it checked.

She had not complained. Not once. She had hobbled on the foot for miles and shaken her head when he had asked her if it was painful. Her lip looked better today, too, and the bruises on her face were harder to see.

He could not imagine one other woman of his acquaintance making so little fuss about injuries and wounds. There was an old square of mirror in the room they were in propped up against a shelf by the door. He had not seen her glance in it even once.

Outside the sounds of the night were receding into silence. He wondered what Wellington must think of such pointless aggression, how he squared off his triumphs with such defeats. He was glad he was out of it now. Once, he had not been.

Once, after A Coruña and Alejandra, all he could think of was going back into battle and losing his life for a cause that was worth it.

He closed his eyes and rested his head against the rough boards that lined the room, her soft sleeping breath coming to him across the space between them.

He couldn't leave her here. At least of that he was sure. If Wellington could not offer her a safe haven, he would take her to England with him. He smiled at the thought, imagining what the tight-laced English society doyens might make of Alejandra Fernandez y Santo Domingo and she of them.

He was certain Amethyst Wylde would like her and Adelaide Hughes. His sister, Christine, would also enjoy the company of a woman who did not simper or flirt or pretend.

His mother, of course, would take some convincing given her loathing of anyone Spanish, but that was a worry for another day.

He laughed to himself, thinking that he had planned out a future for her that she herself had taken no part in. Indeed, she looked as if she would be off in a flash if he did not watch her, gone into the ether and another life that he would have no notion of. Yet with her time in Madrid finished and her safety in A Coruña and the northern coast uncertain she was running out of locations to make a home from.

'You are still awake?' She had stretched out and, in the dark, her lurid hair looked less red. 'It's very late, I think.'

'I like the night. It's the quietest time of the day.'

Without the need to directly look at each other talking was easier.

'I saw a story of you once in an English paper about a girl you were to marry.'

'I didn't.'

'Pardon?'

'I didn't marry her.'

'Why not?'

'I could not give her what she needed.'

Now she sat herself up, her rolled jacket tucked in behind her, and was trying to peer at him through the gloom. 'And what was that?'

'Love. Honesty. Even the truth was beyond my capability. I took the blame of it all, of course, and I think in the end she did not suffer overmuch. Her parents took her off on an extended tour of the Continent virtually straight away and when she returned a good year later it was on the arm of an Italian count who had much in the way of wealth and devotion.'

Alejandra was amazed that he might have told her such a personal thing. She was also unreasonably angry. For him. 'Was your heart broken even a little?'

He laughed at that and shook his head. 'I was relieved. A lifetime is a long while to spend with someone…'

'Who could not love you in the same way you loved them back?' She finished the thought for him.

'Yes,' he said. 'Just that.'

The moments of quiet stretched out, but now it held a lot less restraint and much more warmth, their lines of communication more fluid and real.

'What happened to my signet ring? I left it with the old lady at the brothel and asked her to give it to you.'

This question was unexpected. 'I sold it. Señor Morales was pressing me for the loan repayments and it was valuable.'

'Mateo Morales? The man you thought was me that night in Segovia Street?'

'He is a moneylender and he was going to call in the loans unless I…' She stopped and wished she had not said anything, but he carried on anyway.

'Unless you slept with him?'

'I would have, if you had not come. Do not think that I wouldn't have. I am not the innocent I was before, Capitán.'

His smile surprised her. 'You shot your husband, Alejandra. You knew how to use a knife as you traipsed across the killing fields of war as the daughter of the guerrilla leader El Vengador. What part of that implies innocence?'

'I was not a prostitute then.' Her voice was low.

'And you are not one now.'

'I loved God and Jesus. I believed. I had faith and now I don't. I threw my rosary into the river.' This she said in the hushed tone of the truly dreadful, the worst possible confession she might make.

'Buy another one, then. Begin again.'

She swore. 'The people here, Capitán, those who have been maimed or raped by a force that was supposed to free them, know how impossible it ever is to go back, to be who you were before. The cost of life is sometimes just too much to pay, don't you see? Some things that are broken just cannot be fixed.'

She thought of Ross and the hospital of La Latina, cold and quiet and bare. She remembered walking home without him, the rain in her boots and the tears on her cheeks. Maria had been there when she got back to Segovia Street and she had set a fire and rubbed her feet and put her to bed beneath the warmth of a duck-feather eiderdown, tucked around both slumber and pain.

But she had woken up a different person: harder, angrier, less able to believe in the goodness of anything or anyone.

'How old are you now?'

'Twenty-six.'

'So you are saying that you will be this broken for all of your life. Fifty or so more years of anger and guilt?'

Now, this was new. He was not telling her that what had happened to her was not her fault. No. He was telling her to sit up and take responsibility. And live. Perhaps he was right. Perhaps it was the secrets she carried that kept her from life, the dreadful creeping sadness that had emptied any joy. What was that saying Maria had recited to her on numerous occasions? Shared sorrow is half a sorrow. Perhaps it was the case with the right person?

She took a shaky breath and made herself speak. 'We had a son, you and I, a little boy and I named him Ross. After you. He lived for two minutes and then he simply stopped breathing. The nurse said that happens sometimes when babies are very little because their lungs are not formed or just perhaps because God wanted them back again.'

'God.' His expletive was shocked.

'He had dark hair and he was tiny. Too tiny. He had a purple birthmark on the very top of his left arm, just here, and he was warm when I held him until he wasn't.'

'God,' he repeated, the stillness in him magnified by the night.

'I sent you a letter, with the postage paid through the correct channels of communication. A month later I had a reply back. It said do not write again and that if I did you would set the law upon me for making false claims. It held your seal in wax and your signature.'

He stood and walked to stand by her bed. 'I did not send the letter, Alejandra. I swear it by all that is holy. If you believe nothing else of me, at least believe that.'

'I do.'

The anger in him vibrated, coldly held under control by sheer and utter force. She could see the way the knuckles of both fists were pressed white. 'Ross, you say?'

'Yes.'

'A strong name that claimed his birthright.' There was a catch in his voice, a tremor, each word enunciated with tremendous care.

'He did not suffer at all, at least there was that. He looked just like he was sleeping.' She suddenly wanted to comfort him, this soldier who had fought his way all across Europe and was still fighting, injustice, wrongness, terror. 'He died peacefully in my arms on October the second. At six minutes past eleven at night. It was raining.' Specifics. Details. She remembered each and every one of them as if they had been engraved in blood upon her skin.

'We will bring him home.'

'Pardon?'

'We will bring him home to England and bury him at Linden Park, my family seat at Tunbridge Wells. At least he won't be alone then.'

'You would do that?'

'He is ours, Alejandra. He needs to be with his family.'

Ours. No longer just hers. A shared sadness.

And just like that a dam long held back by hardship and circumstance began to crack; the water at first a tiny drip and then a stream and after a river in full flood and rushing across the bleak landscape of her emotions. She stood, only thinking to escape, but he was by her in a second, letting her cry against his warmth and strength. And she did cry for herself and for Ross, for Lucien and her father and mother and for Spain. For San Sebastian, too, with its deaths and its violence, and for Maria, who had only ever tried to help her.

She could not remember a time when she had done this before, to just let go, no longer trying to control things.

He mopped her eyes finally with the edge of his sleeve, her hair wet, too, from the exertion and her heart sore.

'Who was there to help you, Alejandra?'

'Maria was there after he died and she said that I had only two choices, to go on or not to go on. The brothel needed a younger hand, a steadier one, and I found I was good at the business side of things, tallying the finances and seeing that the house was…in order. Even in a brothel there is some sense of arrangement and structure, you see, Capitán, and it had long been left to run down.'

'You became Maria's right-hand woman?'

'I did and it was an honour. She had no one left and neither did I.'

'And so you wrote the letter for help?'

'No, it was for the truth I wrote. For Ross. Not for me. I wanted you to know that he would be…that he would have a life and a name and a time.'

His ripe curse had her hands rising up to her

chest, about to make the sign of the cross, but she stilled them. To ask the Lord for help now was hypocritical and disingenuous. She could not expect it, not after so long of turning away from his ministry.

'Did you keep the letter?'

She shook her head. 'Everything that I had left of you is gone.' With that she moved away and lay down on her bed, turned towards the wall. She did not want false promises. She did not want him to capitulate only in pity. She was glad when he did not speak again.

When she woke he was missing from the bed by the window, his bag neatly packed and the blanket pulled up. Outside it was blue, the rain and storms across the past few days disappeared and the temperatures warmer again. Hot, in fact, she thought as she loosened the few top buttons on the man's shirt Lucien had given her.

For the first time in a long while she felt hungry, as if she should eat well before greeting the day. Another difference. She folded her jacket into the small sack she carried and put on her boots before washing her face in the cold water someone had left in a china bowl on the table between the beds. Her heel ached and although she had tried to wash it when she could, in both rivers and smaller streams, an inflammation had set in.

Then Lucien was there, offering bread and cheese.

'We can't stay here in San Sebastian. Wellington has his own worries and there are no boats in the harbour to take us north.'

'North?' She could not quite understand what he meant.

'England. You can't go west because of the Betancourts and the south and east are still controlled by the French. We should have safe passage towards Bilbao, though, in the smaller ports on the Costa Vasca.'

'I cannot come with you to England. How would you explain me to your family?'

'We will think on that on the road,' he returned and lifted up his bag. 'When you have finished breakfast we will go.'

An hour later they were riding through the countryside on two steeds Lucien had managed to procure.

The closeness of last night had not been lost

altogether and the tight dread of her life seemed to have been unwound a little. Lucien had not left her in San Sebastian and he had promised to bring Ross home. For that alone she was grateful, but there were other things that ran around her body and in her mind that owed no tether to simple gratitude.

When he had held her last night against him in comfort she had wanted what they had enjoyed on the high passes of the Galician Mountains, to feel him inside her once again, to know the passion and the glory of a connection that she had never forgotten.

She looked away from him so that he would not see that which burnt in her eyes. But when she glanced up at the sun streaming through the trees and leaving beams of light on the air she felt hopeful.

The word surprised her. It had after all been so long since she had once felt that.

Lucien watched the landscape about him. It was still dangerous to ride through these passes without an escort from the military, but Wellington could not spare any men and Lucien did not wish to wait for a week or two until he could.

So he was cautious and wary as the miles passed, checking distance, listening for sounds and watching the horizon for any sign of movement that could be risky.

He felt flattened from her news of their baby son, all his defences down and the loss of what could have been. He was also furious that she had written to him when she was pregnant asking for help and that somebody had sent an answer back refusing it.

His mother, probably. The wrath inside made him shake.

'Where do you live when you are not in London?' They'd slowed the horses to give them a break and so were able to talk.

'At Linden Park, in Kent, to the south of the city,' he qualified as she frowned.

'And your family is there? You said once that there were lots of them.'

'Two brothers and my sister, Christine. And my mother. The estate had been left to run down, so that is why I left the army, to try to build it up again and make it prosperous. I am having some success with manufacturing.'

And he was. The textile business had become most lucrative and the power mills and new technology meant everything could be done faster and better. He had poured what was left of the family fortune into the sector, and so far the odds looked to be paying off.

Business. Profits. Manufacturing. Why was he not asking more personal questions of Alejandra or simply getting off his horse and dragging her into the substantial undergrowth around them to see if they could rediscover all they had felt before? He wanted her with such a violence he could barely breathe and it worried him.

Last night had been a revelation, but he was wary, too. He needed to get Alejandra to England first and home to a place where she would not be able to simply disappear. He no longer trusted that she would not flee in the environs of her own land given that the freedom from Spain's independence was creeping back in.

She had always said she would never leave Spain, but if he brought Ross to England, would that not engender a different loyalty? A base. A place to put down roots and grow from?

He could not afford to harm the small trust

that was developing between them by going too fast, by expecting too much closeness.

Hence he turned the subject to other things.

'When I left Spain after Pontevedra the boat hit a storm in the Bay of Biscay and it took us a lot longer to reach England than Alvarez had imagined. At times I wondered if the ship would not just sink into oblivion.'

'And your wounds? How did you fare by the time you did reach it?'

'Badly. I was ill for a long time and then convalesced at Montcliffe, a friend's family seat in Essex. Daniel Wylde. He was in Spain with me.'

She nodded. 'You spoke of him in your fever dreams at the hacienda, calling him to help you. And of some others. Francis and Gabriel. Like the angels in the Bible,' she qualified and reddened. It was the first religious reference he had heard her make since he'd met up with her again.

'I grew up with them all. Daniel has a wife now called Amethyst and children and Gabriel is married to Adelaide. They are not women who covet society and its frippery.'

The fright and distance in her eyes was evident. Once, he had imagined Alejandra in the city with her bravery and confidence dressed in a fine gown, but now…all he saw was fear and uncertainty, the red in her hair strangely contrasted against the sheen of her skin.

But she had smiled four times today, which was twice more than she had yesterday and four times more than the day before that.

He did not want her to meet his family looking beaten. He wanted her to lift her eyes and become the woman she once had been.

The small port town of Bermeo came into view towards the late afternoon and as luck would have it the tide was in and they managed to find passage to England on a fishing boat that would leave in an hour.

Lucien was pleased to pay the fare and pleased, too, for the hammocks slung on the deck that were to be theirs for the two-day journey. Alejandra had barely spoken to him and he knew without being told that she was more than wary of finding herself in England.

Chapter Thirteen

London

'I did not realise that she was a woman you had strong feelings for, Lucien. I thought she was a charlatan cashing in on a quick way to an easy life, a woman who would hoodwink and dupe you with the threat of a pregnancy. That was what I thought.'

His mother was crying, large tears falling down both cheeks.

'But to never consult me on it. To simply burn the letter and never tell me anything at all? It is that I cannot forgive you for.'

He had confronted his mother about the letter after introducing her to Alejandra. The meeting had been tense and he could see on her face that she had recognised the name. After taking Alejandra to the library and asking the maid to bring her refreshments Lucien had gone back in order to find out the exact story.

'I know it was wrong, Lucien, but you were so sick I thought another problem might simply finish you off. I was going to talk to Daniel Wylde of it, but he was never here in London, what with his leg and the problems he was facing at Ravenshill Manor, and after a time...I felt ashamed. Too ashamed to ever bring it up again even when you were better.'

'She lost the child. Our child. Your grandson. Alejandra named him Ross. He was too little to live.'

A fresh wave of tears had him almost feeling sorry for his mother, but he refrained from moving towards her because the anger that had stifled him all of the journey home was still too raw and fresh to dismiss. He wanted her to be as hurt as they had been.

'Do you think that my reply might have caused...?' She did not finish, her face an ashen white.

Of a sudden Lucien's anger changed to grief and he could no longer say what he thought he might have.

Turning, he simply walked out the door and back to the library. Alejandra was there, sitting on a chair by the fire, and he thought that although it was not very cold, to her it must seem so.

The gown he had found in a shop in Bournemouth which had been serviceable and appropriate there was old and tatty in London. The colour did not suit her, either, the orange against red only bringing out the garishness of both clashing shades.

'She does not like me? Your mother. She did not look happy at all when we arrived. I am sorry for it.'

'Don't be. She is a woman who takes a while to warm to those she does not know. We will leave for Linden Park on the morrow, but you will need a chaperon.'

'A chaperon?'

'In England it is not done for a young unmarried lady to spend time alone with a man.'

'But we have been alone for nearly two weeks now.'

'The very height of scandal,' he returned, 'and better not to mention that to anyone at all.' She smiled. 'My sister, Christine, will come with us to Kent and also my aunt. Mama will no doubt venture down at some time, too, but for now…'

'She was the one who sent the letter, wasn't she?'

He nodded. 'She had a dream I would die in Spain and she thought…'

'To save you from harm. A mother's prerogative, I should suppose, to try to protect her son.'

He shook his head. 'No, it was unforgivable. If she had been honest, I could have been there to help you when Ross was born.'

For the first time since he had found her in Madrid she stepped forward and touched him willingly. One finger placed gently against his lips.

'You are here now. It is enough.'

'Enough for what?'

'For me. This now. For being here with you and safe in England.'

He took her hand and held it to his heart, liking the warmth of it and the littleness. The pulse in her wrist beat fast.

'I am not sure of anything any more, Lucien,' she whispered, but she did not pull away. 'I am not sure of who I am or of what

I might become. I used to be more sure, but now…it is cold in this land and grey and all I can be to you is a…nuisance…'

The last word was whispered as if it were too terrible to say louder.

'I bled a lot when Ross was born and the doctor who attended me at the hospital said…' She took in a breath and kept going. 'He said I would probably never have another child. It could be true.'

The green in her eyes burnt with shame and sorrow.

'So you see your mother is right. I should not be here with you like this…' Her hands ran across the shabby fabric of the dress before rising to her hair, pulled from its fastening after a day's hard ride from the coast. 'I cannot fit in here even if I wanted to.'

As he was about to answer the doorbell rang and voices were heard booming over the silence.

'Where is he?'

'Where's Luce?'

When the door opened, a man and two women spilled into the room.

They were all beautiful. That was Alejandra's first thought. Beautifully dressed, beautifully presented, beautifully English, their manners instantly harnessed into politeness as they caught sight of her standing by the fire.

'You are Alejandra?'

The tall man with pale green eyes came forward first. He limped slightly and had the air of a soldier. 'My God, Luce actually found you? I never thought he would.'

Lucien had now moved over to her side. She felt his presence there and was pleased for it.

'Alejandra Fernandez y Santo Domingo, this is Daniel Wylde, the Earl of Montcliffe, his wife, Amethyst, and my sister, Christine Howard.'

The two women smiled, but there was puzzlement on their faces.

'Is most nice to meet with you.' Alejandra hoped her grasp of English was correct. It had been so long since she had spoken the language aloud with her mother and Rosalie herself had not been in any way fluent.

Both women acknowledged her and then Christine spoke again. 'You are the one who dyed my brother's hair? In Galicia? He cut it off short when he returned to England to get rid of the black and he looked like a scarecrow for weeks and weeks after.'

'Scarecrow?' Was that a good thing or a bad one?

'Espantapájaros.' Lucien supplied the word in Spanish and it fell into the library like an interloper. Every tome here was in English, she'd looked at the shelves when he was in with his mother, and there had not been a single title in Spanish.

'It was a protect,' she qualified, tripping on the last word as Daniel Wylde moved forward and spoke.

'Well, we thank you for it, Alejandra, for rescuing Lucien in Spain and saving his life. He is dear to us, you see, and without him...'

'Is my favour to do. He helps me also from the French. I am agree he is good man.'

Por favor, que me entiendan.

Please, let them understand me.

The words ran under everything she said even as Christine Howard reached out her hand and laid it on Alejandra's arm, her smile warm.

'Do you have other clothes with you? Other

things to wear? My brother is obviously lacking in his duties in finding you such a gown.'

'Lacking?' She did not know this word at all and looked to Lucien.

'Le falta.' A further Spanish translation. 'Don't tell her of the breeches in your bag or the man's shirt.' This was also said in Spanish and very quickly. 'Christine will never let me hear the end of it if you do.'

Watching Lucien Howard at a disadvantage in the presence of his sister made her smile. 'I leave all my clothes in Madrid,' she said slowly and saw the relief on his face.

'Like a red rag to a bull,' Amethyst drawled and everyone laughed.

Why should they speak of bullfighting? Alejandra thought, trying to understand the humour. They were brutal and bloody and she had never enjoyed the spectacle. Surely here in the mannered salons of England such a thing would be abhorrent. She turned again to Lucien for explanation and he gave it slowly in English.

'My sister is a woman with a love of fashion and it would give her great pleasure to help you choose other clothes. It is both her calling and her downfall,' he added and laughed. 'No one ever quite measures up.'

'Ignore Lucien. She has a gift for it, I promise.' Amethyst said this. 'Though I think you will not need much help at all.'

'Except with your hair.' Christine reached out a finger to touch her head. 'May I?'

Bemused Alejandra nodded.

'This is not your natural colour, surely?'

'No. Is dark, not red.'

'Much better then for such a shade would suit your eyes and skin. Did you cut it yourself?'

'Yes. Many times.' She wondered if she should have said that or not, but Lucien's sister seemed most adept at identifying faults. She frowned, too, at the scars on her right wrist as the sleeve of her jacket fell back and even the last remnants of the red paint on her nails was noted.

A poor specimen, she probably thought. Lifting her chin, though, she met Christine's eyes directly and this time real humour marked the light blue. Like Lucien's eyes, only darker, and threaded at the edges in gold. Were the

Howard siblings all as beautiful as these two, she wondered, or as forthright?

'Perhaps we could start now, Alejandra.'

'Start?'

'My room is close and I am certain we could find something more suitable to dress you in. Amethyst will help us, too, and my maid is very useful with a needle.'

Lucien would not come with her, she was sure of it, and the thought made her hesitate. But still this dress was an ugly colour and the shoes were most uncomfortable. If they talked slowly, she would manage.

A moment later she found herself bundled away from the sanctuary of Lucien and his library.

'So the fire was mistaken intelligence, then?' Daniel sat on the chair before the desk and made himself comfortable.

'No. There was a blaze, only Alejandra had not returned from Pontevedra, the port she had taken me to, and so she escaped it. Her father died, though, and the house was razed along with many of the men living there.'

'Was it the French?'

Lucien shook his head. 'It was another guerrilla family who lived close by. Old rivalries,' he explained and poured them both a drink. He would not say anything of Alejandra's first husband or the revenge his death had incited.

'She is very beautiful, your Spanish lady.'

'Yes.'

'And very unprotected. The scandal would be huge if anyone were to find out how long you have been in each other's company. Unchaperoned, I am presuming.'

'It's why I didn't just head to Linden Park from Bournemouth, but came straight to London. With luck no one need know of her past.'

'Where has she been living since you returned if her home was gone? The perpetrators were undoubtedly still on the lookout for her, so I am presuming she had to hide somewhere.'

'In Madrid.' Lucien smiled at Daniel's deductions.

'But she never thought to contact you?'

'No.' He took a decent sip of brandy and swallowed it.

'Because she found another protector?'

Lucien shook his head.

'I am certain she would have had no lack

of men interested in helping her. What did she do for money, then, after her home was gone?'

'She ran a business in La Latina, one of the central barrios in Madrid.'

This time it was Daniel's turn to laugh. 'No wonder Amethyst liked her so much. What sort of business?'

'A brothel.'

'Hell.' He repeated the word again and stood. 'Under her own name? That could be difficult.'

'No, under a different one.'

'Another identity, you mean? A dangerous occupation, I imagine, for a small and beautiful woman.'

'She used the place as a way to extract information from the French customers and move the intelligence on to the British. It was a cover.'

'Even more dangerous, then. Lord above, Luce, she sounds like the perfect match for you. Don't you dare let her get away.'

In answer Lucien simply poured another drink and hoped Alejandra was not going to be too overcome by the ministrations of Christine and Amethyst.

* * *

She had never been particularly worried about her body in front of others and when the maid peeled off her gown to discover nothing at all beneath it, she simply stood in the centre of the room naked.

Christine and Amethyst on the other hand both blushed.

'Oh.' Christine reached for a blanket on the bed and wrapped it around her bare shoulders. 'Well, I think we shall have to remedy your lack of underclothing immediately.'

Lack. *Falta.* Alejandra struggled to remember Lucien's translation.

'Though I must say with a figure like yours you will be a pleasure to dress.'

Amethyst Wylde began to giggle. 'It looks like you go in the sun without clothes, Alejandra?'

She nodded. 'A long time before when I am a girl. Is hot in Spain.'

'How wonderful,' Christine suddenly said. 'I have become so very sick of all the rules in England. Your Spain sounds like just the place to live.'

And then it was easy. Feeling less different and tense, Alejandra began to remember more of her English and reply without so much trouble.

They were kind women, good women, and the clothes Christine took from a wardrobe, which stretched the whole side of one wall, many and of fine quality.

Christine ordered a maid to bring hot water, to which an infusion of lavender was then added. It made Alejandra feel as if she was home again amongst the aloes and olives and lavenders, such water, the feeling growing as a cloth was brought across her body and the grime and sweat from days and days of travel was washed away.

Then there was a linen chemise brought out from a box and wrapped in tissue and a cotton stay was fastened above, her breasts folded into the fabric. A petticoat came next, draped across her bareness, the bodice tight and the skirt generous. The soft feel of silk was wonderful as white stockings with garters of ribbon were pulled to her knees.

'This is just the beginning, Alejandra. Now we must decide on a dress and I am certain that you would suit bold colours in a gown. Like this.' Reaching over for a vivid red dress from her cupboard, Christine peeled away the calico. 'Or this.' Another gown joined the first, royal blue and frothed with lace, and then a third in green and gold.

'They are all beautiful.' Alejandra could not believe the softness of the fabric or the fineness of the stitchery.

'I make them,' Lucien's sister said quietly. 'The Ross estate is trying to gain back what it has lost financially and though Lucien is doing a grand job the money does not yet run to a large budget for gowns and the suchlike. So this is my effort to appear more than we are.'

'You make the dress of yourself?'

'With the help of my maid, Jean, and her mother mostly. But I love the feel of fabric and the possibility. It would be better if you kept that bit of knowledge private, though.'

'To tell no people of your cleverness?'

'The *ton* is a group who believe any labouring should be done by the lower classes. They do not believe a woman should earn money or work a day in her life at any interesting job.'

'Oh.' Alejandra was taken aback by the notion.

'I ran a timber company for years and now we have a most successful horse-breeding business.' Amethyst's words were soft. 'Outside of London one can be just who one wants to. People find their places and no one complains as long as you are careful.'

'And you are?'

'Decidedly.'

It was almost like at the hacienda. There were rules to break and others not to and if one kept inside the forbidden boundaries one could be...free.

Christine went even further. 'My brother is not a man to restrict others in doing what they want to for he himself has lived outside the narrow confines of propriety for years. So talk to him and find your own pathway here, Alejandra, and you might be surprised and delighted with what you are offered.'

Turning, she brought the green-and-gold gown away from its hanger. 'But for now we need to make you look unmatched. Firstly, though, we must do something about your hair.'

Lucien could not believe that Alejandra was the same woman Christine and Amethyst had whisked away two and a half hours earlier.

Gone was the shabby orange gown that had drooped across the neckline and sagged at the back and in its place was a stunning green-and-gold creation that held a froth of lace on its bodice, highlighting the rounded swell of bosom and velvet skin.

Her hair was different, too, the strands wrapped across each other and secured in curls and waves around her face, giving the impression of its previous length and shine. It was no longer the gaudy red, either, but more like the hue he remembered.

However, it was the look in her green eyes that had changed the most, for the ragged urchin of wariness and carefulness was replaced by a woman who was beautiful. And she knew it.

The words she had given him years ago on the high hills of the Galician Mountains came to mind. Many men have liked me, she had said, and even then he could well believe it true.

But now? Like this? God, she would stand out in society like a rare and exceptional jewel. The very thought was enough to bring him to his feet.

'We will leave for Linden Park in the morning.'

* * *

Lucien Howard did not like her transformation for some reason. The frown on his face was deep and he looked anywhere but at her as he spoke of his plans for moving south to his family seat in Kent.

Perhaps he thought her murky past might catch up if they stayed in London or maybe he was ashamed of her lack of English. Whatever it was he did not say a word about the things his sister had done to make her look…better. His friend Daniel Wylde, however, was more than effusive.

'You are a magician, Christine. My wife is always saying you are such and today proves it. The men of the *ton* will be champing at the bit when they see you.'

'Champing…?'

Lucien leant forward to explain. 'They will lay their hearts at your feet. Beauty holds a great deal of sway in London society and a woman here barely needs anything else to flourish.' His words were laced with irritation and also tiredness.

They had hardly slept since they had left Spain and he'd had a lot less sleep than she.

Every night on the boat in her hammock when she had awoken in the dark he had been there, sitting and observing the horizon to keep watch.

She had napped, too, for a good many miles as they came north from Bournemouth in a hired coach, where a doctor had been summoned to see to her foot in a private room at a tavern on the way. The medic had not been gentle. The pain of his ministrations and the effect of the brandy Lucien had offered to dampen the agony had left her exhausted and she'd slumbered in his arms as they had wended their way up to the city of London.

But now here with her foot feeling so much less painful, and her hair and clothes so very fine, she wanted Lucien Howard to recognise the difference, to see her as she once had been many years before, the only daughter of a wealthy and noble Spanish family with a generous dowry and all the chances in the world to marry well.

Half a lifetime ago. The elation dimmed somewhat as she counted back the years. Perhaps this new persona was as false as the last one with the lacy gloves covering the scars on her right wrist and a dozen silver bracelets. She knew Christine and Amethyst had seen the old wound on her left thigh, too. They had looked shocked at the sight before hiding it, but this damaged woman was her as well, marked in danger, formed by war and honed in shame.

'We will come down next week, Lucien, to see you. There is a man in Orpington who has a fine roan mare for sale that I wish to take a look at.'

Daniel Wylde's voice cut into her thoughts.

'We will bring Adelaide, too.'

'Is she still running her clinic in Sherborne?' Lucien asked this, interest in his eyes.

'Yes. Gabe is having a lot of success in new practices of farming and they are halfway through rebuilding Ravenshill Manor. If he can get away we could bring him down. Francis may be able to come, as well.'

Friends, thought Alejandra. Daniel. Amethyst. Christine. Gabriel and Adelaide. Francis. She could not remember a time when she had even had one true confidante her age. A fault that, probably. Another lack her life was full of. England seemed to underline all that she was not.

When she saw Lucien observe her with concern in his face she smiled, a brittle pretend grin that felt wrong in its falseness, but it was suddenly all that she had left. She was adrift here as surely as she had been in Madrid, the future uncertain and the past defining her.

She was glad when the others gave their goodbyes and left, the concentration needed for speaking a language she was not fluent in exhausting.

'They are good people, Alejandra. Real people.' He looked at her with question in his eyes as she raised her left arm, the silk tight against her skin.

'But where does a knife fit in a sleeve such as this?' Her leg bent next. 'And what manner of woman could ever escape quickly in these shoes?'

'It is seldom one has the need to whip out a knife in London, but be warned. Words are the choice of weapon ladies and gentlemen of the court use and they can be as cutting.'

'And therein lies the problem. I can barely understand a simple sentence, let alone one that might slay me.'

He began to laugh. 'Beauty is enough here, believe me. Just let that do the talking.'

'You think that I am? Beautiful, I mean?'

He stepped back and nodded, though the same wariness she had seen before was more than apparent.

Hope rose inside her breast and into her throat, making her swallow away tears, the pale blue of his eyes touching her in all the places she wanted his hands to be. Strangers and lovers. And friends, too, once. The sun slanting in the window frosted his hair with gold and silver.

'If people here were to ever know who I had been...' She left the rest unsaid.

'Scandal has its own deficiencies. If you don't care enough about the gossip, it is fairly self-limiting.'

'Like you don't...care, I mean, about what others say?'

He smiled.

'I doubt whether the girl who watched me walking along the paths of lavender at the hacienda of her father would have given it a second thought, either.'

'I am not certain if that girl was ever real, Capitán.'

'No?'

'Once, I was braver, but loss has the tendency to take that away.'

'To live is dangerous, Alejandra. And to love.'

She was silent. *It was. It once had been.* Here in London he was far more the earl than just a plain soldier and anything between them before was now caught in such a difference.

The perfume Christine had applied most liberally was strong and she had the beginnings of a headache that made her feel slightly nauseous. The love of a man. The love of a child. The love of a country. Each one of these was fraught with the possibility of loss and each one of them had been snatched away from her so very easily.

There was still the problem of his mother, too. She did not wish to be the reason for some difficult family rift. Her own had been the masters of that particular downfall.

But Lucien was looking at her as if she were beautiful and unflawed and honourable and when he stepped forward to take her hand she felt the same shock of awareness she always felt when he touched her.

'Take a risk,' he said quietly. 'Take a risk, Alejandra, and live.'

And so she did, moving forward, feeling his warmth and then his hand lifting her chin, the pale eyes close and questioning. Only now in a world of books and silence, the sound of breath, louder, raw, desperate, and his mouth then against her own, slanting, wet and hard.

Her neck arched and she opened to him, his tongue and teeth upon her, no small query now, but only taking. She could barely breathe or think, the weightless truth of wonder and rightness.

Home. With Lucien.

Her own hands came up to his hair, threading through the gold, entwined and pressing close, and the old magic that had got her through four years of hell returned, roaring against weakness and replacing doubt.

She loved him. She did. She had loved him from the very first second of finding him unconscious on the high fields of battle. A connection, a communion, a man who was her other half of living.

Take a risk and live, he had said.

She pulled back a little and looked him straight in the eyes.

'I will love you for always and I will never stop.'

'Marry me, then, Alejandra. Be my wife.'

She was speechless, shock tightening her throat as tears welled. She allowed them to fall down her cheeks and on to the green-and-gold silk of her beautiful gown.

'Yes.' No thought in it save delight and hope.

And then it was easy kissing, soft and honest, quiet in the way of disbelief and wonder. He would be hers for ever as everything and everyone else had not been, her husband, her lover, her friend.

'You are certain?'

'More certain than I have been in my entire life. Right from the beginning it was only ever us.'

'Us,' she whispered back and, standing on tiptoes, she found again the warmth and sweetness of his mouth.

Lucien wanted her. It was all he could think of. He wanted to be inside her. He wanted to know the pounding fury that had haunted his every moment since their trysts on the road down into Pontevedra from the high hills of the Galicians. Every other woman ever since had been irrelevant and shadowy and he had struggled for four years with intimacy and honesty and desire.

His member was rock hard against her, the physical embodiment of his desperation, and he did not try to hide it. He could not. He pressed against her and let her feel the extent of his need even as his hand slid beneath the green-and-gold silk of her bodice, undoing the buttons and cupping one round and full breast.

'You are mine, Alejandra, and I will be yours, too, for ever.'

In answer she simply pulled the gown from her shoulder and allowed him everything.

He suckled hard and felt her gasp, but he could no longer be careful. His teeth closed over the nipple and her nails scraped down the back of his neck, drawing blood, he thought and smiled.

They would mark each other again as they had done before, in ownership and in power.

Already the red whorls of where his mouth had been were drawn into her skin.

He wanted to lift her up and take her to his bed, through the corridors of the town house, past his mother and his family, ignoring all of them to assuage the pounding beat of his heart that drummed in his ears.

But he could not because by doing so he would ruin his one chance of getting it right this time, of doing it properly, of cherishing her and protecting her in all the ways that he had failed to do so before in Spain.

He did not want another child out of wedlock, either. He wanted his friends there to witness his wedding and his mother watching to understand the love he brought to his wife. He wanted it beautiful and honest. He wanted to say their vows in the Linden Park chapel in front of God because he knew right there and then that Alejandra needed that. She needed to be back in the fold of religion in order to be whole. And so did he. With family and friends. Together.

Repositioning her bodice, he brought her in against him and took a breath.

'When we are married we will finish what

we have started here. I promise. I want to be married at the chapel in Linden Park and the ceremony shall take place as soon as the banns are read and a dress is made.'

'A dress?'

'I hope the Church of England is suitable for you, my love, for this time we will be wed by the grace of God. This time it will be perfect.'

Dinner that evening was a strange mix of elation, tension and shame. Lucien's two younger brothers were at the table as were Christine and his mother.

The Countess of Ross had been crying, Alejandra could tell, and she held herself stiff and silent as news of the forthcoming wedding was given by Lucien.

Christine was the most excited, all her chatter about the gown she would design and of how she had seen a picture of a beautiful woman in Boston with exactly the dress she could imagine Alejandra in. The boys watched her covertly, blushing when she glanced at them and hardly talking.

Young men were always simple, she thought

to herself and smiled as Lucien took her hand there at the table and held it firmly.

'We will be married at Linden Park in the chapel. We do not wish for a big wedding, but the Wyldes will come as well as the Hughes and Francis St Cartmail. And all the aunts, of course.'

'What of the Bigley cousins and the Halbergs? You will have to ask the Kingstons, too, for they would be most upset if they were not invited.' Christine chattered away and the list of potential guests became larger and larger until Lucien drew her ponderings to a close.

'We will have who we want, Christine, and that is the end of it.'

'And the banns will need to be posted?' This was the first thing the Countess had offered all night.

'I will make certain they are when we go down to Linden Park tomorrow.'

The older lady nodded and twisted the kerchief that she held in her hands this way and that.

'Are you of the Anglican faith?' This question was directed at Alejandra.

'No. I was Catholic, Lady Ross.'

Christine frowned. 'Was?'

'I have not much being in church for few years.'

'Because your faith was tested and found wanting?' These words came from Lucien's mother and they were barely audible.

'Tested?'

Lucien translated and the silence about the table was heavy.

'I did believe. Once. I hope this will come again.' It was all she could say with any sense of truth.

'I hope so, too.' The Countess gave these words with a great sincerity and Alejandra smiled at her. Perhaps things would be all right one day between them. She could only hope.

When the meal was complete Lucien excused them both and took her out into the small garden behind the house. It was a warm evening, the promise of a late summer in the air, and bells rang from somewhere close.

They came together easily, his arms wrapped about her.

'I want you so much that it hurts.' No pretext. No hidden meaning. She felt that want, too, and bit down on it.

'How long?'

'Three weeks.' He knew exactly what she meant. 'I have to go north for a few days this week for there is business that needs my attention after being away for so long.'

'Of course.'

'It might be better, too.'

'The distance?'

'The temptation,' he returned and kissed her hard and quick before moving back. As he turned she saw the marks of her nails across the skin at his nape.

'It will be a church wedding?' She had been surprised when he had said that at the table given what he knew of her faith. 'I am not entirely sure I should even be in a house of God, making promises.'

He began to laugh. 'Mama betrayed me in the worst way possible and she is at the chapel most days. Christine shared a bed with the man who was supposed to be marrying her, but he died instead, and I have killed more people than I can even remember and yet I am not rebuffed. What exactly is your crime, Alejandra? What is so terrible about what you have done?'

'I have given up on God,' she returned without a second's thought.

'Yet he brought you to me, to love again. Perhaps after all he did not give up on you.'

'Lucien?'

'Yes.'

'Never leave me. Not ever.'

'I won't, my love.'

Chapter Fourteen

There were white roses on the end of every pew and more in large vases by the pulpit with blue and yellow ribbons tied in generous bows. Christine's work, Alejandra supposed, nothing left to chance.

Her dress floated about her legs, the soft blue silk embellished with flowers, and in her hair was a garland of fresh white rosebuds.

But it was Lucien she looked at, standing tall and still at the top of the aisle, Daniel Wylde beside him. He was dressed today in unbroken black and it made the pale of his hair lighter and even more beautiful. His eyes were full of promise as he watched her walk towards him and when she reached him he held out his hand.

And at that moment with the sun coming through the stained-glass windows in slivers of colours and an organ playing a hymn she knew and loved; with the scent of rose petals and the warmth of family and friends all around her, Alejandra felt a shifting, an easing, the warmth of belief coming back into her heart like magic. Celestial magic. Unexplained and beautiful. She could even feel Rosalie there beside her and her father and Maria and Tomeu and Adan. And Ross in the strength of Lucien's grasp and in the love on his face.

Perfect. This was a perfect moment that she would never forget and God had given it to her. After all the sorrow and hurt there was wonder again and grace.

Lucien had known it with his insistence on such a wedding, celebrated with all that was good in the religious form and in the Church of England.

She was home. Here. Understood and known. When the music ceased she looked up into his eyes and smiled.

'Thank you,' she whispered.

'You are welcome, my love.'

Only now. Glancing at the minister, she gave him greeting and waited for the service to begin.

* * *

She was suddenly nervous, more nervous than she had ever been. He had not seen the scar on her thigh, not properly before, and it had been a very long time since they had last come together. Her wrist, too, was something he might ask about and there were marks across her stomach that had not been there last time.

Ross.

This was another fear. A baby or the lack of one. She could not quite come to terms with whether she would want to be pregnant again or would dread it.

It was late now and she had left Lucien downstairs in the large drawing room at Linden Park. Everything about this place was huge. The house. The gardens, the staircases, the ponds. Even the bed behind her. Their bed now, a large four-poster with a draping of gauze around every side of it.

The only small thing was the wisp of lace nightgown Christine had given her for her wedding night. She wondered if she should be wearing it at all as it reminded her a bit of the clothing in the brothel on Segovia Street.

Another worry loomed. What if that was all

he could remember? The drugged and angry Antonia with her lewd actions, cut-glass earrings and blood-red hair.

She glanced in the mirror and was momentarily heartened.

Her locks now were so much darker and shinier, a result of a shampoo Adelaide Hughes had concocted for her in her house in Sherborne and a good-quality hair dye. She had been eating better, too, and the thin angular bones of Spain had been softened somewhat here into more feminine curves.

Lifting one finger, she carefully touched the diamond ring Lucien had pledged his troth to her with. Substantial and permanent.

It was all enough. She was enough. Footfalls on the boards outside had her glancing worriedly away from the mirror.

And then he was there, completely dressed, the dark of his clothes a contrast against the pale of her lacy white nothingness. He held a small box in his hands and he gave this to her without touching.

'For you, Alejandra.'

She had not thought to buy him a gift. Was this an English custom that was expected?

But when she opened it she forgot about all her fears and gasped in delight.

'A rosary?'

'Of jets. I found it in a shop on Regent Street and thought of you. Like your old one, if I remember correctly, the one you used constantly in Spain.'

'The one I draped across your chest as we took you from the battlefield.'

'The one you brought with you on the march west to take me to the boat. It was always so much a part of you I thought you ought to have a replacement.'

'It is beautiful.' The beads slid through her fingers in the same old familiar way, the words in her head as they always had been and joy in her heart.

'I will treasure it.'

'Oh. I nearly forgot,' he suddenly said. 'My mother also sends you this.' Digging into his pocket, he brought out a small fat statue of polished jade.

'What is it?'

'A fertility god from the ancient Chinese, but she swears it will work. She had six children and her mother had seven and they all attribute such abundance to this.'

'It is an old heirloom, then.'

'Indeed.'

'She wants us to have another child?'

'She most certainly does. She believes she had some hand in Ross's death and blames herself for it.'

'She shouldn't. He came too early. I do not think anyone could have stopped that from happening.'

'Would you tell her that, perhaps, when you feel ready to?'

'Yes.'

'Would you tell me it, too, over and over, so that I might know...?' He stopped and she heard the tremble of self-blame in his voice, the first time ever she had heard him anything but certain.

'Make another child with me, Lucien. Tonight. So we all can live.'

God, she was brave, Alejandra, his wife. He noticed the pulse in her throat was fast and shallow and yet still she would offer him absolution and forgiveness.

The lace nightdress she wore was very little. He could see the scars on her wrist and the larger one on her left thigh. He had touched the raised skin before once when he had taken her on the coastal path less than an hour before they had been parted in Pontevedra. He wondered who had hurt her so badly. Her first husband, probably, but the hacienda had been a dangerous place, too, as had the brothel in La Latina.

He needed to be gentle with her, but already a desperate need was rising.

He hoped they might have a child and that there would be something left of them when they had gone, but if they could not, then that was fine, too. He had Alejandra, finally, bound by law and church to him. For ever. It was enough.

Reaching out, he ran a finger across her cheek and then down her neck and on to her shoulder. The same awareness he always felt when he touched her made him smile. She had filled out, her curves more noticeable in the month since they had left Spain. Her hair had grown a little, too, reaching past her collarbones now, a curtain of shiny dark silk.

'You are so very beautiful,' he whispered, and she leant in to kiss him, on his cheek, on his chin and then on his lips, her mouth finding him with her tongue. No quiet kiss this, but a full and sensual onslaught. He was completely dressed and she was in less than nothing when one of his hands threaded between her thighs and came into her secret place with a hard intent.

She groaned and arched her head so that her eyes fell into his own, sparked with desire. He could see his movements in the verdant green, flickering as he pushed deep and her swollen flesh opened further.

'Love me, Lucien,' she murmured, her hands now at the buttons of his jacket and then his shirt. The neckcloth was unwound and his trousers fell.

He stepped out of them and lifted her, legs wound about his hips keeping him close, and then the softness of the mattress was beneath them, the thread work of the quilt under his knees. Pulling the gauzy hangings around the bed, they were caught in their own private space, the candle blurred and the fire a soft glow across the room.

He could no longer hold back, he needed her with the sort of desperation that held no stopping. Opening her thighs, he simply plunged in, the wet warmth welcoming and tight.

Their breathing was louder now, hoarse in the quiet and building upwards to the place where release came quick, beaching waves of pleasure cleaving them to the other and claiming what each craved, made one by the ecstasy. Alejandra shook afterwards when the tightness had waned, shook in his arms and tipped her head to his.

And this time when he kissed her it was quiet and gentle, languid and heavy, open-mouthed and closed. They were still connected, still joined, the seed he had spilled thick inside her and the last shuddering spasms of muscle not quite yet gone.

Taken. His. Even the thought kept him hard and he pushed in with purpose.

'Again?'

He nodded, his hand wrapped around her buttock as he lifted her against him, changing the angle, and when she finally cried out with the relief of orgasm he simply covered her mouth and took the breath of her to mingle with his own.

* * *

She felt heavy, swollen and full, the small wisps of lace torn from her body with the movements of their lovemaking so that what was left of the nightgown lay limp on the counterpane of bobbled silk.

And she still wanted him. Inside her. Pleasuring her in that particular way he had that defied all she had ever known of sex. She was a wanton. The thought pulled her lips upwards and one hand fell across her breast, a budded nipple hard between her fingers.

Then his mouth was there, suckling, using her breast as a babe might as she held him tight against her, fingers threaded through the hair at his nape. She wanted to nurture him and feed him. She wanted to bring him into herself where no one else might touch them and where they would never again be apart.

There was pain there, too, and she relished it when his teeth grated across the softness because it told her she was alive and here and protected. She leant across him and bit him on the shoulder, not quite drawing blood.

Then he was above and turning her, drawing up both hands and tethering her small fingers with his own.

Helpless surrender. He took her exactly as he wanted and she loved every moment of it.

Roughness had a different appeal to the soft and in it she felt the loosening of her past, the brothel, the deaths, the danger. She was small and he was large. He was pale and she was dark. He was hard and she was soft. She relished the differences as he showed her the mastery of his sex.

And afterwards he knelt between her legs and used his mouth to soothe her, to cool her, to sup at the well of womanhood as only a husband could do, healing the anger, accepting the past.

A lesson in loving that wrapped about her heart. Pain had many names, she thought, and one of them was Lucien. If she ever lost him again, she would die.

She woke in the night late and disorientated. Lucien stood against the windows, looking out, though he turned as soon as he perceived her watching him. His body looked like a statue of burnished marble, an erection stiff against the moonlight.

When she joined him he came into her from behind, their reflection surreal. It was cold against the glass, her breasts against the shiny hardness making each nipple bud. He did not hurry, either, but changed the rhythm of his penetration just as she was getting used to the last one. To lengthen the timings. To heighten the need.

'Please?' she whispered.

'Wait,' he said.

'Now?'

'Soon.'

And then it was there, intense and fragile, the wrenching truth of the together plucked from apartness as she felt his seed within and his teeth at her neck.

'I love you, Alejandra.' The words shivered across her nakedness and fell into the dark.

'How did you ever find me in that prison in Madrid, Lucien?'

It was almost dawn and the few hours of sleep they had managed was enough to allow them comfort.

'I knew the French used the place for interrogations and I'd found an old copy of the plans in the reading room on the Paseo de Recoletos. I was there every day waiting for you to come, so I had a good many hours to look.'

'You thought I would be caught?'

'Well, if I had heard the rumours of a woman who stole the French secrets, then I was certain the French would soon be likely to, as well. Nothing is sacred in the cut-throat world of espionage and so I felt it would pay to be prepared.'

'It was still a risk. Even with all that preparedness.'

'A risk I am glad I took.'

'I thought I would die. I thought they would rape me, too. I was not at all certain that when they did I could keep quiet, either.'

'You might be surprised at that. After a certain amount of pain it all begins to feel the same.'

'It was like that with your back? The scars are fierce still.'

He laughed. 'I do not even have the inclination to remember them, Alejandra. It is finished with, that time, and I am thankful.'

'Only now?'

'England is a quiet place and many here don't like to be reminded of the chaos in other lands. I have not shown anyone save the doctor my scars.'

At that she laughed. 'Your sister and Amethyst were not particularly worried to see the remnants of the wound on my thigh.'

'They each have their own skeletons, though. It is those who have never been touched by strife or war who make the most fuss.'

'Juan tied me to a horse and dragged me around a field. The root of a tree gouged my leg.'

The shockingness of it fell into the room like a stone, but she wanted to tell him of it all. He deserved to know.

'I was too independent, he said. Too inclined to do what I wanted. He needed me submissive and docile. My father found me in the back room of Juan's house. The wound had festered badly, you see, and I suppose Juan was ashamed of being such a bully. He did not allow anyone near me and I got sicker and sicker.'

'Then I am glad you are a good shot. The bastard deserved what was coming to him.'

'Tomeu gave me the gun. It was my job to see him punished, not my father's.'

'I knew I liked him.'

Alejandra snuggled into the warmth of her husband. 'You see, that is why I love you. You allow me to be me.'

Reaching over, she picked up the rosary from the bedside table and cradled it in her hands. 'I shall say a Hail Mary for Juan Betancourt and forgive him because otherwise…'

'You never forget.'

'Will they accept me, do you think, as your wife? Those in society, I mean. I should not wish to make it difficult for you to go to London.'

He shrugged his shoulders and laughed. 'After last night, Alejandra, nothing you could ever do would make it difficult for me.'

He couldn't get enough of her—that was the trouble. He could barely breathe properly when he was away from her and the duties of his earldom and manufacturing business had called him to London three days this week alone.

Their nights were what he lived for, losing himself inside of her, two becoming one as the long summer nights shortened and the first coolness of autumn appeared.

Tonight they had walked to the lake that stood in front of Linden Park and made love in the boathouse at the end of the pier. With the water lapping around them and the moonlight on Alejandra's naked body, Lucien brought her on to his lap and wrapped the blanket around them both, her legs to each side of him.

A quiet coupling, watching each other as the rhythm quickened, seeing the love in her eyes and the smile on her lips.

She was so very beautiful, her breasts moving with his pushes as nipples tightened by want. Soon he would suck them and she would whisper into his hair with soft words of Spanish. Protecting him. Wanting him.

He wondered what it would be like when her breasts were filled with milk and her belly lay swollen with babe. He wanted lots of babies, lots of family, the final expression of their love made physical. But even if they could not conceive he would be happy. With her.

When he smiled she saw it.

'You are happy?'

'I am,' he returned.

'With this?' she questioned, tipping her hips.

'Are you?'

'In the brothel I felt sick every time I would have to go into the room of a French soldier, to search his clothing, just in case something went wrong.'

'Did that ever happen?'

She shook her head.

'But with you…with you I don't think.'

'You just feel. This and this.'

'And this,' she added, her tongue winding around the lobe of his ear and down to the nape.

Chapter Fifteen

'There is a problem, Luce.' Daniel leant forward in the leather wing chair where they were tucked into an alcove in one corner of White's on St James's Street a month or so after the wedding.

Lucien frowned and finished his drink. 'What is it?'

'The brother of Sir Mark Walters has been telling all who will listen that you cohabited together outside of wedlock as you travelled from Bournemouth to London.'

'And how does he know this?'

'He was there as you landed from Spain, Luce, and he recognised you. It seems he is an artist of sorts and fashioned a drawing. A picture has just been published in a tatty broadsheet and it has had numerous reprints.'

'Do you have it?' Suddenly Lucien knew exactly what the problem would be. Alejandra had been dressed in her lad's clothes as he had carried her to the conveyance at the dockside because her foot was too sore to walk.

'I do.' Daniel brought forth a sheet of paper and unfolded it, the faded lines taking nothing away from the rendering.

'Hell.'

The drawing was every bit as damning as Lucien thought it might be and it was verified as the truth by Viscount Radford, a man who held no love for the Howard family.

'Damned if I admit this and damned if I don't? Can it blow over?'

Daniel laughed. 'Everything can eventually blow over, I suppose, but the fact that you might spend the next years as outcasts is one you might consider. Especially if you have children.'

'Has Amethyst seen this?'

'She has. She said when she was vilified by the *ton* over the furore of her first husband she was glad we all stood together. You are surrounded by friends with lofty titles, Lucien. Perhaps you should use us.'

'Beard the lion in his lair, you mean?'

'Your sister can have us all looking most presentable and Gabriel has already sent out the invites to his ball. A venue, so to speak, that is neutral and sympathetic. He could make certain the doubters are there.'

Leaning back, Lucien pulled his hands through his hair. 'I don't know if Alejandra is ready for this. If she is vilified anyway...'

'Then you are in exactly the same position as you are now and at least you will know what you are up against.'

'I'd like to hit Walters and Radford right now. Hard.'

'Which would be playing right into their hands and everyone will think it true.'

Daniel was right. He had to be cleverer than that. He had to laugh at the accusation in such a way that people would begin to question its validity. Alejandra looked less and less like the girl he had found again in a Madrid brothel and more and more like the well-born lady that she was.

If they all stood together, it might work.

He just had to convince his wife that the charade was actually worth it.

* * *

Alejandra was sick when he arrived home from the city and lying on the bed in their room, a cold flannel across her brow and the curtains drawn.

He had never seen her look so lifeless before and pulled up a chair in front of her. Had she heard the rumours already? He was pleased when she smiled and sat up, her arms wrapping about his neck.

'I missed you, but I think I must have eaten something last night that did not agree with me for I have not been feeling well. How was your day?'

'I saw Daniel at my club.'

She frowned and pulled back. 'Is there something wrong, Lucien?'

'This.' Leaning back, he took the broadsheet with their likenesses from his bag and laid it out on her knees.

'He is an accomplished artist, unfortunately, Mr Frank Walters, the man who drew this. If he'd been less talented, it may not have mattered. His friend Viscount Radford is verifying his story and he is the son of a man who felt my father duped him in a business venture.'

'And it does? Matter, I mean?'

'I'm not sure. If we do nothing, it might just go away.'

'Or it might not?' She took his hand in hers and he liked the warmth. 'So you think attack is the better option? It's fight or flee?'

Lucien laughed. 'Nothing that dramatic, thank goodness. He can't touch us here in Kent, but…the *ton* has strict punishments for those who might flout their rules, Alejandra, and pre-marital sex is one of the big ones.'

'But we didn't… Not that time…' She blushed and stopped.

'You were unchaperoned. That is enough. If we do go to Gabriel's ball, though, as we had planned to, Daniel and the others will stand with us.'

'In support, you mean?'

'With my family title and with the Hughes' and the Wyldes' and St Cartmails' support, too, it might well be enough to put this to bed so to speak. Besides, we are married now and so as a scandal it is not as juicy as the one that would have ensued if we were not.'

'How many people will be there?'

'Most of the *ton*, I should imagine. Gabe has a wide and varied circle of friends.'

'I thought you said they did not go about in society much?'

'They don't. This is the first ball I have ever been to at the Hughes family home.'

The warmth of her skin drew him closer and he pulled off his boots and jacket and joined her on the bed. With Alejandra's head against his chest and his arms about her shoulders he felt whole again, the ride home from London worrying and long.

'I wanted to be home,' he said after a moment or two. 'It seems when I leave you all I can think about is when I am coming back.'

At that she pushed herself up and faced him directly, her hands around the sides of his head and a smile on her face that held more than humour. 'I have been waiting for you, my love, and it has been a long day. Shall we shorten it?'

Her fingers went to the fall of his trousers and undid the buttons, and then the warmth of her fingers was against his flesh.

'Whatever happens out there in the world will never harm us, Alejandra. I promise you that.'

'I know,' she replied and then her full lips came down across him.

The next morning Alejandra felt a little better, though she was worried and shocked by the drawing and by such a blatant attack on their relationship. Lucien's mother and she were just starting to be civil to one another, the deathly silence that she had endured since coming to England finally punctuated by one or two warm smiles. What would an older lady think of this now? She felt for the rosary in her pocket and ran the beads through her fingers, asking for guidance.

They would have to chance on a good outcome from Gabriel and Adelaide's ball. She knew they would have to because otherwise there would always be whisperings and conjecture. After a life of such things she wanted only harmony and peace, to just fit in here without troubles and gossip.

Lucien beside her was still asleep, the dawn light across his hair marking it with gold. They had woken in the night and made love again, so the bedding was tousled and heaped about them and she felt wanton and languid.

With care she traced the line of his cheek and he woke immediately turning towards her, his pale eyes focusing into alertness as he spoke. 'For many years I have come from slumber into hardship and now…now all I have is beauty.' He reached for her hair and slid his fingers down the length of it. 'I'm glad it's no longer red.'

'I hated the colour. I hated everything about those years without you. There was only loneliness in Madrid and the flavour of grief. If anything is allowed to threaten us…here…' She could not go on.

'You have been worrying?' He stroked the lines on her forehead with one finger. 'And nothing can ever part us again, I promise you.'

'That is what I loved about you right from the beginning, Lucien. Your certainty. I felt safe and safety is an underrated commodity, I think. You realise this only when you have lived through chaos. So tell your sister, then, that she needs to fashion a dress for the Hughes ball that will make me look magnificent, like Boadicea going into battle.'

'You are sure?'

'With you beside me, Lucien, I can do anything.'

She liked it when he gathered the length of her hair in one hand and came across her. No small loving this, no fragile tryst. Throwing away problems, she savoured the warmth and the strength of him and forgot the world around them altogether.

Two weeks later Alejandra sat in the carriage and took in a deep breath as the conveyance slowed in front of the Hughes town house. They were late.

'Everyone will be there waiting for us. Don't worry.' Lucien drew back the curtain and looked out into the night.

They were to have met at the house of Daniel Wylde, but the wheel axel had been loose on the carriage on the way up from Linden Park, so they had had to wait at a tavern in Southborough until it could be fixed and made safe. By the time they had got to the Ross town house to get ready for the ball everything was a rush.

Closing her eyes against the traffic and the lights, Alejandra fingered her rosary and prayed that the evening would be a success.

'It will be fine, sweetheart.' Lucien was in black tonight, the colour of his clothing unbroken save for the snowy-white neckcloth that he had folded carefully and the paleness of his hair. 'Give them five minutes and they will love you like I do.'

But she could not be consoled by his words, she who had ridden into battle and roamed the high and dangerous passes of the Spanish mountains, she who had understood the intricacies of knife fighting and swordsmanship since she was a young girl. Alejandra Fernandez y Santo Domingo, daughter of El Vengador. No, in England the enemy was different, less seen somehow and thus more brutal. Here she could rely on neither her prowess nor her reputation. Here they could deny her and Lucien a place in society and a home in London and gossip was a vice that went on and on. For ever, if those who hated them should so wish it.

'And if they don't? If we fail…?'

'I never fail,' he returned, and the look in his light-blue eyes was exactly the one she had seen in the olive grove above the hacienda as he had walked himself almost to death to try to get fitter.

Reaching for his hand, she was glad to feel the warmth of his fingers against her freezing ones.

'Look at it like a contest, Alejandra. Two steps forward and one step back. We will never win them all over, but we just need enough.'

The chatter rose on the air as they walked to the top of the stairs, hundreds of people below in their very best attire and candles in holders along every wall and horizontal space.

'The Earl and Countess of Ross.'

The major-domo announced them, his formal tones booming across conversation, and the lull was almost instant. Every face turned their way, every eye, the silence deafening as they walked down the wide long staircase into the room proper.

If Lucien had not been beside her, she would have fallen, she was sure of it; as it was she tripped slightly and he held her still.

'Put your chin up and smile. We are married.'

And she did, simply looked the spectators directly in the eyes and smiled as if all she expected were compliments and wishes of good luck and good fortune.

Her heart still pounded in her chest and her stomach trembled with nerves, but she did not show it.

What was it her father had said once? *Attitude is all in the confidence, Alejandra. People will believe of you what you will them to.* Her mama, too, as she had brushed out her hair at night gently and lovingly. *It's not what you look like, my love. It's what's inside that counts.*

Well, inside was steel and tenacity and the will to survive. She had survived all that life had thrown at her so far and she would not allow this wonderment with Lucien to be snatched away on the flighty tail of gossip.

If they hated her, then they did. If they were harried from the society, then they were. But she had her husband at her side, close and solid and menacing.

And there were others, too, Gabriel Hughes and his wife, Adelaide, and Daniel Wylde and Amethyst. Christine was there, too, and then there was Lucien's mother walking towards her and taking her hand in her own and holding it close.

'Welcome to the family, Alejandra. An apology is too little a thing to offer in mitigation for what I have done to you, but here my name carries considerable weight and so I add it.'

'Thank you.' She held her mother-in-law's fingers and smiled.

And then it was easy, the whirl of faces, the greetings, the quiet introductions and the dancing, with Lucien always beside her, his hand on her back, guiding. When the musicians came back to their seats for another set of dances he leant down and whispered quietly, 'It is a waltz, Alejandra. Will you dance it with me?'

'I am not practised in any way,' she countered, but he stopped her.

'Let me lead and it will be simple.'

She felt his heartbeat, saw his long pale hair rest against the blackness of cloth and the small lines of laughter that ran about his eyes.

Beautiful. As beautiful as the first time she had ever met him up in the after smoke of battle by the aloe hedges. A whole history together, good and bad.

'You never doubted that this would work, did you?' she whispered as they came together, close.

He shook his head. 'After I thought about it I realised that you have the sort of beauty that draws people to them, Alejandra, and in your red dress. Well…'

He stopped for a moment before continuing.

'I used to imagine you in this, you know, even when I was sick after A Coruña. I knew in this colour that you would be unmatched. And you are.'

'Only because of you, Lucien. All of this is only because of you.'

Adelaide took her hand as they walked into supper, the quiet beauty of Gabriel's wife undeniable.

'I am so glad you were able to come, Alejandra. Gabriel was adamant that we have at least one grand ball in our life, though I am hoping that it will be the last.'

'You do not enjoy dancing?'

'Oh, indeed I do. What I don't enjoy is all the fuss of it and the necessity to be so well dressed and so very uncomfortable. Oh,' she suddenly said, digging into her small beaded reticule and bringing out a small bottle of powder. 'I have something for you. One teaspoon each morning for a week is what I give to every new wife for fertility and well-being. The power of it comes from belief,' she added, 'but I have heard that the Spanish people have a healthy love of folklore, so I am certain it shall work very well on you.'

'Thank you.'

'It is good to have you here and to see Lucien happy. He has not been, you see, for so long. Gabriel was certain that he was lonely, though I think he had plenty of chances to remedy that as the ladies here are more than forward and he is very good-looking.'

Beautiful.

Alejandra imagined him coming back to England after A Coruña, sick and hurt and sad. Such dark days for them both, caught in war and fire and death.

'I will never let him be lonely again,' she promised and meant it.

Adelaide smiled. 'Amethyst said that I would like you and I do.'

Half an hour later Alejandra walked down a small corridor to the retiring room. She needed to take a break for a moment from all the well-wishers and those asking to be acquainted with the new wife of the Earl of Ross. The evening had been such a mix of dread, nerves, wonder and elation she also needed a moment just to stop.

She was surprised to come across a man tarrying to one side of the retiring-room door.

'You may have fooled them all, but you cannot fool me, *señora*, for I know who you truly are and if it takes me a lifetime to prove it, then so be it.'

'It was you who made the picture? You are Frank Walters?'

He shook his head and began his tirade anew. 'No, I am Viscount Radford and you are a disgrace to all of womanhood if you think you can get away with such utter lies simply by appearing here on the arm of your husband this evening. You ought to be ejected summarily from society and asked never to return for you corrupt the innocence of all women...'

Such vitriol shocked her to the core, though he spoke in such rapid English Alejandra could barely make out the sense of his words.

He was close to her now, the hate in his eyes fierce and unguarded, though as he raised his arm as if to strike her the patience in Alejandra broke completely and she blocked his hand with her own, bringing his arm behind his back in one quick motion and pulling up.

He groaned and she was glad for it. With only a little push she could snap his arm in two places. It would be so very easy to do so.

'Perhaps, *señor*, is not good such hate. I can hurt you, but I think you are not worth that bother.' Jabbing her elbow into his back, she let him go.

'Stay far from me and my family. If you come near me again, my husband will kill you and I am not stop him. Do you understand?'

For the first time fear lingered where hate had been and Alejandra was pleased for it. She watched as the man almost ran in the opposite direction before leaning back against the wall.

'Did he hurt you?'

Lucien materialised from the gloom and stood there watching her.

'You heard?'

'All of it. Shall I kill him now?'

At that she smiled. 'No. I do not think he will trouble us again.'

'Good. Then are you ready to go back to the ball?'

He did not admonish her or even question

her about what had just happened. He had allowed her the right to defend herself in the way she knew how and backed up her actions. If she had asked Lucien to kill Viscount Radford, she imagined he would have. Quietly. Efficiently. Without any fuss or problem whatsoever.

A man she could trust. A man who understood she was not as other women here were and yet admired her for it. He was not asking her to change in this marriage. No, he was allowing her to walk beside him equally. A partnership based on strength.

'I thought perhaps we might leave soon. It is not late, but…' The lines about his eyes creased into humour.

'I would like that.'

Threading her arm through his, they turned together to find their hosts.

Once back in their bedchamber at the Ross town house he peeled off the red gown with a careful slowness, the silk running through his fingers and pooling at her feet. Then he removed her underclothing.

'You are so very lovely,' he said when the layers of lawn and silk had finally gone, Alejandra's velvet skin burnished by candlelight. A short string of pearls at her throat caught the light and he unclasped these, too.

'I think it is the gown, Lucien. A dozen people asked me tonight who my dressmaker was. I said Mon Soeur was the label and that I should send them the card of calling on the morrow with the name of the seamstress upon it.'

'Christine?'

'She does not wish for anyone to know she designs these dresses, so I do not quite know what to say.'

Lucien began to laugh. 'I am surrounded by women who are not as they seem.'

'That is because you are comfortable in your own skin, my love. A lesser man might be threatened by it.'

'And a lesser woman would ask incessantly for my help.'

'Your friends all admire you. Do you know that? Each one of them at different times has approached me and made certain that I know what a treasure I have been given and each one of them has intimated you were lonely. For all the years of our apartness.'

'I was.' He brought her into his arms. He had removed his own jacket and shirt and neck-cloth now, though he still stood in his trousers and shoes. 'They all tried to match me up with this person and with that one, but it was only ever you…'

'Only us, Lucien. You and me.'

'Only now,' he agreed and lifted her eyes to his. 'When and where was the engraving done on the inside band of my signet ring?'

'In Vigo. I went there after Pontevedra when you did not come and paid the last of my money to a jeweller to inscribe the message. I knew I was pregnant, you see, and I thought if anything happened to me, then our baby would need to find its way back to you. To family.'

'Oh, God.'

'It was stolen, though, in the house in La La-tina. How on earth did you find it?'

'An English soldier had a run-in with a homeless man in Madrid and recognised my crest. He brought it home to London and gave it to me.'

'So you knew I was alive then, instead of gone in the fire?'

'I hoped so, but Luis Alvarez's son confirmed it for me.'

'You went back to the little port of Pontevedra?'

'Xavier Alvarez, Luis's son, told me you had sat on the wharf for a long while after his father and I left and that you had been near to crying. He then said he saw you take the road into the hills and it was raining.'

He stopped for a second and took in a deep breath. 'The timing would have been too tight. There was no way you could have reached the hacienda by the time of the fire. If it had not rained? If you had not tarried? If you had taken the coastal road…?' His voice shook with all the possibilities that had not come to pass.

'You think I cannot say exactly the same of you, Lucien? If you had not come to the French prison and helped me escape, if you had not made your appointment in the brothel under the name of Mateo, if you had not been fighting in A Coruña in the first place.'

'But I did.'

'And we do,' she whispered, her hands across his chest and then falling downwards. 'Only now, remember. If we live like that for all our lives, everything will be perfect. The future will take care of itself and the past is finished with. We cannot change it. All the best intentions shall not undo it.'

'Only now?'

'This moment. This second.'

He stepped out of the last of his clothes and brought her up against him hard.

'You are my world, Alejandra.'

And then they forgot to speak at all.

Afterwards they lay entwined in a tangle of sheets and quilting, close and quiet. The last of the four-hour candle had burnt down the wick, sending dark smoke into the air and strange reflections on to the ceiling.

'My mother would have liked you, Lucien. She would have been pleased with my choice.'

She felt his chest shake in humour. 'Who was she, your mother?'

'Rosalie Santo Domingo y Giminez was the daughter of one of the wealthiest landowners in Galicia. Papa and she were betrothed under the old system of marriage. He was strong and a leader of men and my mama's father admired him. Europe was being cast into war and chaos and I suppose her father thought Enrique Fernandez y Castro could protect both his daughter and them, protect their inheritance and land and cattle. As it happened my grandparents were both taken by sickness one winter soon after the marriage and everything went to my father, the new groom, and the outsider.'

'So no one was happy?'

'Well, my mother certainly was. She saw how Enrique could rally people around a cause with his logic and his menace and she understood that allies at a time of great change were more than useful. Within two years he had the pledges of thirty other landholders around us for help and loyalty and he never looked back.'

'Did Rosalie?'

'No, not really. She hated the violence and the fighting, but by then she had lost her heart to him as well as all her property. Women lose their rights under marriage, you see, and my father was a great believer in that particular concept. And so here I am as landless and moneyless as my mother was in the end, for I doubt that even if peace comes to Spain I will be able to regain possession of our lands and houses.'

'I did not marry you for your money, Alejandra, or your lack of it. I married you because I love you. Besides, my interests in manufacturing are starting to pay off and I would say by the end of the year the Ross finances will be more than healthy again.'

Relief made her breathe out heavily. 'So you were not in need of a wealthy heiress?'

'No, I was always in need of a beautiful and brave Spanish warrior.'

'Are you in need now?' She smiled and turned towards him, her hips lifting against his side as her mouth came down across his own.

She was sick again in the morning and as she returned to the bed Lucien pulled back the sheets and took her into his warmth.

'Could you be pregnant, Alejandra?'

The shock of the words kept her still as she counted back the days since her last menses. She had never had one moment of sickness with Ross and so the thought of it had not even occurred to her.

Lifting the sheet, he traced the outline of her nipples. 'They are darker, sweetheart. Is that not a sign?'

'I don't know. I can't remember from before…'

'And you have been tired.'

'Yes, but I thought it was the listening to
English and trying to understand it all the
time.'

'Perhaps you might talk with Amethyst and
ask her about the signs, or Adelaide.' His hand
spread across her stomach now, in possession
and in hope, she thought, too.

'Mama was not a woman to speak of these
things and I have never had another to ask.
Maria was older and forgetful and the one child
she'd had was dead, so I didn't like to question her.'

'What of the other girls at the brothel? Surely
there were babies born there?'

'Indeed there were, but I was their employer.
It was not appropriate to ask them.' She sat up
suddenly, unable to lie there any more. 'Could
we go to see Amethyst or Adelaide?'

'Now?'

'Yes. Perhaps it is true. Perhaps I could be…
We could be parents.' Her hands came across
her mouth. 'Do you think it could be true?'

He pushed back the bedcovers and offered

her his hand. 'I am a man with absolutely no idea of anything to do with pregnancy, but let's get dressed and go.'

Chapter Sixteen

All his best friends were here in the library at Linden Park—Daniel, Gabriel and Francis—waiting with him amongst the books and brandy for the birth of his and Alejandra's first child.

The doctor had been called a good hour ago and the midwife had been here most of the morning. Amethyst, Christine and Adelaide had insisted that they stay with Alejandra, too, and for that Lucien was extremely grateful.

'It's always exhausting, Luce, this waiting,' Daniel said. 'God, I remember it with the birth of Sapphire. I thought that neither my wife nor baby would live beyond the hour and that I'd be alone for ever and…' He stopped and finished the last of his brandy.

'I think Lucien would rather hear the good

stories, Daniel.' Gabriel voiced his opinion now. 'The ones that speak of women having a baby one moment and getting on with their lives the next.'

'In America the Mohican women would depart alone to a secluded grove near water to prepare for delivery.' Francis's remark was soft and Lucien looked at him in amazement.

'You think it would help my wife to be outside by herself trying to have our baby?'

'No. I am just saying that birth is often relatively painless and simple.'

'Keep away from Alejandra until she has had the baby, then. I think she might very well kill you right now if she heard you saying that.'

'Amethyst believes mankind would be doomed if males were the ones who had to give birth.' Daniel spoke again now, more careful with what he said.

Lucien simply paced from the open door to the windows and back. It had been all of three hours since he had last been allowed into the birthing room. How long did these things usually take? He screwed his fingers through his hair and closed his eyes.

If he lost Alejandra again… No, he would not even entertain such a notion.

Opening his eyes, he glanced over at Gabriel, whose small son was almost two now, but who had stayed largely silent in the discussion.

'When Adelaide had Jamie, were you afraid, Gabe?'

'More scared than I have ever been in my entire life. I think it's normal.'

'We had another child. A little boy.' The words were out before he could rethink them, falling into the silence like bullets. 'He only lived for a few minutes.'

'My God.' Daniel stood at that and joined him by the window. 'Was this in Spain, Luce?'

'After I left her in Spain. Five years ago.'

'Alejandra had him alone?'

'Yes.'

'Well, now she has us all. A whole lot of people who can help her and get her through. And get you through, too. In an hour you will be the happiest you have ever felt in your life. I promise you that.'

'What was the name of your son?'

Gabriel asked this question and Lucien was

glad to bring his name here into the room as a part of a waiting family.

'He was named Ross.'

'A good name. A family name.' Francis now lifted his glass and raised it to the room. 'To Ross. May he never be forgotten.'

They each drank deep of their tipple and for some unfathomable reason Lucien could almost hear his little lost child tell him that this birth would go well, that there would be a baby who would grow up as he had not and that all would be better this time around. Lucien smiled. He had begun the arrangements already to bring the tiny body home and Alejandra had overseen the planting of olive, aloe and oak saplings in a grove by the lake at Linden Park. Familiar trees. Small whispers of Spain.

He made himself sit down and take a drink and was just about to swallow the brandy when the door opened.

'Your wife wants you, Lucien.'

It was Amethyst and the smile on her face was wide.

Alejandra was lying in the bed in a nightgown he had brought for her a few weeks ago in London and her dark hair was streaming down over her shoulders. In her arms was a small bundle wrapped in the soft white woollen blanket his mother had crocheted all through the months of winter.

Adelaide stood to one side of the bed next to his sister, the midwife and the doctor talking quietly in the corner, though both looked up with a smile as they saw him enter.

He crossed the room and took the hand that was held out.

'We have a little son, Lucien. Well, not so little really. The doctor said he is healthy and beautiful.'

Through the swaddling clothes a tiny face peered, eyes a dark strange blue and his skin reddened.

'He was born twenty minutes ago and he is breathing all by himself.' At that she carefully placed the bundle into his arms and Lucien felt the lightness and the heaviness all at once as a great surge of love came across him.

Theirs. For ever. A son.

'We had said we would call him Ross, but when I look at him I think he is his very own person. What was your father's name?'

'Jonathon.'

'Then let us name him Jonathon Enrique. For my papa, as well. For the future and the past.'

'I like that. Do you, Jonathon?' he murmured, and one tiny hand curled around his finger, grasping hard.

Family and home had a particular feel to it that was unequalled. So did parenthood.

He brought his wife's hand to his lips and kissed her fingers.

'Thank you, Alejandra.'

'You are welcome, Lucien,' she gave back. 'Perhaps the others might come in now to meet the newest of our families.'

* * * * *

Look for the next in Sophia James's
THE PENNILESS LORDS *quartet.*
Francis's story is coming soon.

MILLS & BOON®

HISTORICAL

AWAKEN THE ROMANCE OF THE PAST

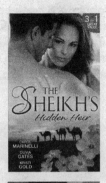

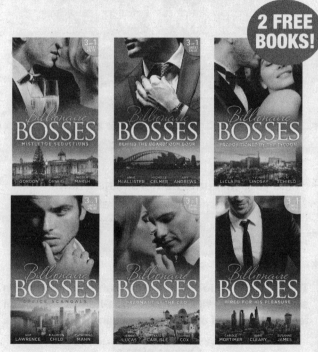

MILLS & BOON®

Why shop at millsandboon.co.uk?

Each year, thousands of romance readers find their perfect read at millsandboon.co.uk. That's because we're passionate about bringing you the very best romantic fiction. Here are some of the advantages of shopping at www.millsandboon.co.uk:

* **Get new books first**—you'll be able to buy your favourite books one month before they hit the shops

* **Get exclusive discounts**—you'll also be able to buy our specially created monthly collections, with up to 50% off the RRP

* **Find your favourite authors**—latest news, interviews and new releases for all your favourite authors and series on our website, plus ideas for what to try next

* **Join in**—once you've bought your favourite books, don't forget to register with us to rate, review and join in the discussions

Visit **www.millsandboon.co.uk**
for all this and more today!